*A Cornish Christmas
at Pear Tree Farm*

A Cornish Christmas
at Pear Tree Farm

Angela Britnell

Where heroes are like chocolate – irresistible!

Published 2022 by Choc Lit Limited
Penrose House, Crawley Drive, Camberley, Surrey GU15 2AB, UK
www.choc-lit.com

A CIP catalogue record for this book is available
from the British Library

ISBN 978-1-78189-515-3

Printed and bound in Great Britain
by Clays Ltd, Elcograf S.p.A.

*To my dear friends Glenys, Pauline and Mervyn
without whose help over the past year I would've
never got this book written – they went above and
beyond to ease my stress over having to sell a house
in Cornwall from four thousand miles away!*

Acknowledgements

I want to express my gratitude to all members of the armed forces who are serving or have served their countries in the past with honour. Many of them won't be home for Christmas this year and far too great a number have left behind a permanent hole in their family's celebrations.

I'm also supremely thankful to the amazing Tasting Panel members who were happy to return to Pear Tree Farm for the festive season along with all of my lovely, loyal readers and give Ashley and Crispin their well-deserved chance at happiness: Steph Price, Celia Bourgi, Gill Leivers, Carol Dutton, Rosie Farrell, Cheryl Woodbridge, Liana Vera Saez, Lisa Vasil, Amy Nordon, Joy Bleach, Carol Botting, Jo Osborne, Honor Gilbert, Lynda Adcock, Fran Stevens, Lorna Baker and Sharon Walsh.

Chapter One

Crispin stared in dismay at the huge banner strung between two poles on either side of the farm gate. The big red letters announced that today was the *FIRST ANNUAL PEAR DAY*, something the swarms of people jostling past him were clearly interested in experiencing. He'd accepted that things would've changed over the last year but it still jarred him.

'Oops! Sorry dear.'

Someone bumped his backpack and a pair of familiar bright blue eyes zeroed in on him as he jerked around.

'Oh my God, you lovely boy. You came back!'

'Hello, Polly. You're looking good.'

'Like the new hair?' His old friend patted the bright orange bun balanced on top of her head. 'It's my autumn do. I might add some black streaks for Halloween next week.'

'It's unique.' *Like you*, he thought. It was a standing joke that Polly's husband Jack never knew what the woman sharing his bed on a Friday night would look like after her regular weekly hair appointment.

'Are you out of the army? Are you tired? Where've you been? Why didn't you tell us you were coming?'

He didn't attempt to answer the rapid barrage of questions because, in her typical enthusiastic way, Polly hadn't stopped to draw breath.

'Everyone's going to be some pleased to see you.'

'I'm not stopping. Just popped in to say hello, that's all.'

Polly scoffed and steered him through the gate. 'Have you got somewhere else to be in a hurry?'

'Not really.'

'Didn't think so. Now we *should* find Nessa first, but I expect she'd still indoors feeding the baby.'

'Baby?'

'You'm some out of touch, aren't you?' Polly chuckled. 'I'll fill you in on all the news later. We could go up and see Jack – he's doing the kiddies games in the upper field – but I've been out to buy more milk so I need to get it over to the tea tent.' She hoisted up her bright red canvas shopping bag.

'Why don't I drop off my backpack and have a wander?' Crowds of people were milling around, there was a table set up outside the farmhouse selling hot pear cider and the sound of live music drifted down from the campsite. 'How long is all this going on?' Crispin must have failed to hide his distaste because she flashed him an indulgent smile.

'It'll be over by about seven o'clock. Stick your bag inside our place and make yourself a quiet cuppa.'

'Thanks.' Crispin swallowed the lump in his throat. He'd never forgotten the kindness of the special people who'd rescued him at his lowest point and gave him breathing space when he'd nowhere else to go. 'I'll catch you later.'

'You'll have to be speedy.' She showed off her bright orange trainers. 'These give me wings. Byeee.'

He ploughed through the hordes of visitors to reach Polly and Jack's bright pink VW camper then stopped outside to breathe in the fresh salt-laced air. The familiar scent seeped into his blood and he dared to think he might not have made a mistake after all.

Ashley swept a hand over her damp forehead. She doubted today's temperature made it to fifteen degrees, but she'd worked up a sweat helping Jack with the children's games. It'd been an exhausting couple of hours attempting to keep the peace between kids arguing over who got the closest on a bean bag toss, and she'd caught one little girl cheating on the lucky dip by sneaking back in a prize she didn't like and swapping it for a different one.

On days like this it was hard to believe she'd only been in Cornwall for about eighteen months; her life back in Tennessee seemed part of another lifetime. Ashley spotted the top of her brother's dark head over the crowd and smiled at Ward's determined stride. No doubt he was making a beeline for the farmhouse, antsy because he hadn't seen his wife and new baby son for a while. Little Tristan was only six weeks old but had them all wrapped around his ten adorable tiny fingers.

She glanced towards Polly and Jack Green's famous pink camper that'd been standing, so she'd been told, in that same spot for over thirty years since the couple came to Cornwall on holiday from Birmingham and never left. Her heart leapt in her throat as she noticed a man dressed in camouflage gear and carrying a bulky backpack hovering outside the Greens' door. The stranger sneaked a glance behind him then leapt up the wooden steps, opened the door and slipped inside.

The whole Pear Day concept was Ashley's idea, and she decided then and there she wasn't allowing any no-good yob to spoil it.

Without stopping to think, she grabbed a thick stick off the ground and crept across the grass to sneak up the camper van steps. 'Don't move!' she shouted and flung the door open. 'I've called the police.'

'I certainly hope you haven't.' The man straightened up from filling the kettle at the sink and swung around.

Now he'd shed the backpack and his coat, the sight of his thickset, muscular physique sent a flash of panic swooping through her. Ashley gasped for breath as the camper closed in around her.

'It's all right, I'm not going to hurt you.' He strode across the narrow space and prised the stick from her iron grip. 'We'll breathe together.'

She couldn't place his deep, soothing accent because the Brits had more of those than a country this size had a right to, but her shallow, jerking breaths stretched out as the panic receded.

'How about a cup of tea?'

'Tea?' A strangled laugh escaped her tight throat. 'Do you always offer people a cup of tea when you're robbing them?'

'I've done a lot of things in my life and not all of them admirable but I've never robbed anyone.' A mischievous glint sneaked into his dark, hooded eyes. 'And even if I was a thief, strictly speaking I wouldn't be robbing *you* because this isn't your home.'

'I know that but it belongs to my good friends, and you've no right to be here.'

'Uh, actually I do. Polly and Jack are old mates of mine and she told me to help myself to a cup of tea. Feel free to check.' His stare intensified. 'Now I get it. It's just clicked where I know you from. You're Ward's sister, aren't you? The American who married Nessa? You had red hair last time I saw you. Blonde suits you better.'

'Oh my God, you're the army guy.' When she'd first

arrived in Cornwall, her brother told her about the Welsh ex-soldier who lived year-round at Pear Tree Farm rent-free in return for his work around the caravan site. Later it emerged that he'd deserted from the British army.

Ashley had only met him for a few minutes over a year ago at Ward and Nessa's engagement party. That was when he'd made the decision to turn himself in, and she recalled feeling a fleeting sense of kinship because she'd been experiencing her own rough time. His rugged good looks had stirred something in her then and were having the same effect now. 'It's Crispin, right?'

'Yep. Crispin Davies. You're Ashley—'

'Spencer.' She'd reverted to using her maiden name after her divorce.

'Do you want to change your mind about that cup of tea?'

Ashley shook her head. 'I hate the stuff.'

'I'm sure there's water in the tap.'

'No thanks. I'd better be off, I've got work to do.' It struck her she was being ungracious. 'Look I'm really sorry about—'

'It's okay. Honest. You were brave and looking out for Polly and Jack. I could've been the local axe-murderer.' A brief smile twisted the corners of his mouth. 'Not that there is one, as far as I know.'

'I'm relieved to hear it. I'm sure I'll see ya around.' Ashley made a quick retreat and didn't stop until she was well away from the camper van.

Chapter Two

'Are you still here, lovey?' Polly popped her head in around. 'Couldn't face the crowds?'

'Not really.' Crispin shrugged. 'You want to give me the rundown on everything now?'

'We can do that walking around.' She fixed him with a firm look. 'You've no reason to hide. I've spread the word already, so we'll say a few quick hellos and, after all the visitors have gone, we're throwing a barbecue to welcome you back.'

Crispin choked on a surge of emotion.

'No argument? You've changed.'

'I'm working on it. How about you give me the condensed version while we're traipsing around and save the juicy details for another day?' He followed her out.

'You're a naughty boy.' She linked her arm through his and they set off at her usual brisk pace. 'Ward and Nessa got married on New Year's Day, and by the time they came back from their honeymoon in Tennessee little Tristan was on the way.' She chortled. 'Didn't waste any time, did they?'

'No reason to I suppose.' Crispin stopped to stare at a sign outside the walled garden advertising various homemade pear products for sale including jams, pickles and even hand cream. 'Business is good?' When he'd left the campsite was struggling to make a profit, but Nessa had been full of plans to turn things around.

'Yes, the garden-to-table courses are a big success.' Colour bloomed in Polly's thin cheeks. 'I do all the cooking.

All vegetarian and organic.' She giggled like a schoolgirl. 'None of Jack's cremated sausages for our fancy guests.'

'Do you still hold your regular barbecues in the summer?' Every Thursday the Greens would host a get-together for everyone staying on the site. He'd avoided them like the plague.

'We don't have time.' A touch of sadness sneaked into her voice. 'Life moves on. Things change.'

'You're right about that.' They kept going and reached the entrance to the upper field. 'Wow.'

'Bit different, isn't it?'

The rough ground had been cleared and a new gravel path ran through the middle of the field, branching off when it reached the top over to three smart wooden buildings on wheels that were all painted in soft earth colours. 'What on earth are those?'

'Shepherd's huts. Well, a modern version of them. The original ones were used by shepherds who needed to stay out in the fields in lambing season. They're the in thing now.' Polly beamed. 'We bought them three months ago and they've been full ever since. They'll be closed up next week for the winter but are fully booked for Easter already. They were Ashley's idea. Ward's sister? Do you remember her?'

'Vaguely.' He hated lying but suspected the American woman might not want him to mention their recent encounter.

'She's a real go-getter. Pear Day was her idea too.' Polly's smile broadened. 'But don't hate her for that.'

Crispin had the sinking feeling he wouldn't be capable of hating Ashley for anything. It'd been a long time since he'd allowed himself to be interested in any woman but something about her wouldn't leave him alone. 'Let's go and see Jack first.'

'Come on, Ash. Stay for the barbecue,' Ward urged. 'Crispin's a good guy and Nessa's over the moon that he's back. There's no need for you to rush back to Tregereth. You've only got a couple of guests in so Lowena can manage fine.'

'I know that – she could run the country standing on her head.'

'But?'

She'd been as shocked as anyone when her brother had left Nashville and gone on holiday to Cornwall early the previous year to see where one of their ancestors had come from and, out of the blue, bought a large neglected house next to Pear Tree Farm. He'd drawn a line under his former country music career and made a fresh start by turning Tregereth House into a boutique bed and breakfast establishment and glamping site. Ward had talked her into joining him because he needed her hospitality business expertise, but also to help give her the courage to leave her domineering husband – thankfully now ex-husband.

They'd brought Nessa's highly efficient and capable sister, Lowena, on board to do the cooking and help with the housekeeping, and Ashley now considered the rather prim and proper Englishwoman a true friend. They'd found a common bond when they were both going through painful divorces and were also very much in sync when it came to a love of organisation and putting abundant energy into their work.

She folded another of Tristan's miniature onesies and added it to the pile. *New babies go through more clothes in a day than I do in a month.* 'I've had enough today, okay? I'll be glad of a quiet evening.' Ashley held up a pale blue outfit with writing on the front. 'I love this. Did Mom send it?'

'Of course.' A broad smile creased her brother's face. 'Made in America with Cornish parts. No escaping the fact he's a honeymoon baby!'

'Have Mom and Dad decided to come for the holidays?'

'What do you think?' Ward chuckled. 'They can't wait to see Tris, and getting to enjoy his first Christmas will be the icing on the cake.'

'I guess you and me are way down the priority list now?'

'Oh yeah.'

Thankfully, it seemed she'd steered him away from discussing the barbecue. She'd no desire to meet Crispin Davies again today.

'Where is our little star anyway?'

'Nessa's getting Tris settled for a nap in his pram so we can walk him up in it later.' Ward gave a wry smile. 'With any luck he'll wake up as soon as the food's ready so I'll have an excuse to walk him around instead of choking down Jack's overdone sausages.' Polly's husband was a sweet man but had a bee in his bonnet about not serving undercooked meat.

Ashley moved the stack of tiny clothes to one end of the cluttered kitchen table. 'I'm heading off.' She hugged her brother. 'I'll see you tomorrow?'

'Yeah. The forecast is dry so I'll be up to cut the grass.'

Somehow her brother juggled taking care of a lot

of the outside work plus the financial accounts for both businesses, usually with a smile on his face.

'Things are winding down now. Our last garden-to-table classes are next week. The shepherd's huts are shutting down for the winter and we've only got a few caravan bookings over the next month, then we're done until Easter.'

The seasonal mentality of the tourist industry here had taken her a while to get used to after working in a large city hotel back in Tennessee. She and Nessa had a few clashes when she enthusiastically shared her brainwaves about how to turn Tregereth and Pear Tree Farm into more year-round businesses. Her sister-in-law insisted that people worked non-stop from Easter onwards and were ready for a break by October but also used the winter to make repairs and alterations without guests under their feet. Nowadays she shared her ideas like a dripping tap rather than Niagara Falls.

Ward draped an arm around her shoulder. 'Off you go and get back to plotting out our next great project with Lowena.'

'Plotting?'

'I'm not complainin'. Without the two of you I'd never have got the business off the ground, and you know damn well I'll probably agree to whatever you dream up next.' He shooed her away. 'Off you go, kiddo.'

Not long after her brother bought Tregereth House, he'd waxed lyrical over the phone to her that the short walk from the old house down Penmeor Road, past the entrance to Pear Tree Farm and on into the small village of Polgarth, was one of the things that convinced him he was making the right decision. Tonight, as she did it in reverse, it was too dark to see the expansive view over the lush Polgarth Valley, but the soft air laced with a hint of salt from the sea a couple of miles away still enveloped her with a welcome sense of peace.

She strolled past the lanterns glowing on either side of the new wrought iron gates Ward had specially commissioned to fit the property, crunched her way up the gravel drive and pushed open the front door.

'I've got a lovely chicken casserole ready.' Lowena scurried out of the kitchen with a big smile on her face. 'Come in and put your feet up. You must be tired! We'll open a bottle of wine while you tell me how Pear Day went.'

'It was great and it gave me another awesome idea. What do you think of a series of Cornish-themed festive weekends – highlighting local crafts and foods?'

'I love it.' Her bright blue eyes sparkled. 'Can't wait to hear more.'

Summer visitors only? Rubbish.

Chapter Three

Crispin stretched out in the bed and wondered when he'd got so soft. When he'd arrived last week, Nessa had talked him out of pitching his tent and it'd amused him when she'd taken her time deciding which caravan would suit him best. Years ago, she'd named and selected the outside paint colours for all of the vintage caravans on the site based on her favourite summer songs and ice cream flavours. After a great deal of thought, Nessa plumped for "Mr Blue Sky" as his new residence because she claimed the rich dark blue paint matched his eyes, and the lyrics of the famous ELO song referred to a blue sky that came out of hiding – rather like him. He'd spent almost three years on the run from the army after his last tour in Afghanistan, most of it living in his tent here at the farm. Nessa flat out saved him, gave him back his dignity and never once asked awkward questions. Ward Spencer was one lucky man.

He threw back the covers and ambled out through the narrow passage to the kitchen. Crispin took his time over cooking and eating his breakfast, then fixed another mug of tea to carry back with him to the bedroom. Once he was showered and dressed, he made his bed with knife-edge corners and did a sweep right through the caravan, tidying away anything out of place. *Old habits die hard.*

Today's cerulean-blue sky and mild temperature made it perfect for working in the walled garden. When he nervously asked about the possibility of getting his old job back, Ward almost fell on him with relief.

'That'd be awesome. I've managed with help from Jack

and hiring the occasional part-timer from the village, but it's been an uphill battle.'

Crispin fetched his tools from the shed and worked on hoeing the weeds between the rows of kale, cabbage and leeks. He automatically started to sing while he dug. The ingrained love for the Welsh hymns he'd grown up with had thankfully never left him. Next, he needed to fix netting over the winter salad leaves to keep the birds away. All of a sudden someone behind him started clapping.

'That was incredible. Jack overheard you singing once and tried to tell me you've got an awesome voice. You've put Tris to sleep.' Nessa's hands rested on the baby strapped to her chest. '"Bread of Heaven", isn't it? I remember hearing that in church with my mum and dad when I was little.'

'We call it "*Cwm Rhondda*".' He cracked a smile. 'Hear seventy thousand Welshmen singing that at Twickenham for the rugby and you might think you're in heaven already – especially if we win.' A painful memory slammed back, and he struggled to hide the emotions sweeping through him. One evening in the mountains outside Kabul they were gathered around a campfire after a makeshift meal. Everyone had been in a sombre mood because they'd lost several friends that day in an ambush. He'd found himself singing that same old hymn because the lyrics gave him comfort on a day when it'd been in short supply. By the time it finished, he hadn't been the only one swiping at his eyes.

'Ward should hear you. He hasn't had any time to spend on his music since Tris arrived, but I bet you could get his creative juices going again.' She rubbed Tristan's back when the baby started to stir. 'You'd enjoy hearing the mining songs he wrote last year. One of the folk groups has taken them up and performed them locally.' Nessa's eyes shone. 'The Wheal Boys are singing at the pub here in Polgarth on Christmas Eve. Maybe you'll come?'

'Maybe.' The direction of the conversation bothered him. 'I should get back to work.'

'I'd lose my head if it wasn't fixed on.' She laughed. 'I almost forgot why I came up here in the first place. If what you're doing now can wait, there's another job I'd like you to do.'

'Not a problem. What do you need?'

'They're doing a Halloween thing tomorrow at Tregereth.' Nessa rolled her eyes. 'It's another of Ashley's bright ideas. She needs hay bales moving around and goodness knows what else done. If you could help Ward out, that would be great.'

'Of course.' That shot down his plan to avoid the intriguing American woman but he couldn't say no. He'd do the job and get out of there as quickly as possible.

Ashley was on a high. She loved seeing her plans come to life, and after the roaring success of Pear Day, she was now working full tilt on tomorrow's Halloween celebration. She'd been fascinated to discover many of the traditions she grew up with originated with Irish and Scottish immigrants who brought their old customs surrounding the Celtic festival of Samhain across the pond with them. The trick or treating custom probably evolved from Celtic supernatural beliefs that led people to offer food or drink to the fairy folk in Ireland and the piskies in Cornwall. The immigrants adapted the turnip lanterns of their native lands by using the easier to carve American pumpkin. Apple bobbing was a safer version of a Cornish game that scarily involved grabbing apples from strings suspended from a cross decorated with lit candles. Obviously, there hadn't been any health and safety regulations in those days.

There was a rap on the kitchen door and she set down the apple she was working on. Already this morning she'd washed and dried a hundred red apples and was almost done with sticking a wooden lolly stick in each and setting the fruit on sheets of parchment paper, ready to be covered in toffee.

'Do you want to supervise the maze building, Ash, or you gonna trust us to get it right?' Ward's eyes, the mirror-image of their father's, sparkled with good humour.

'Us?'

'Yeah, I've got a helper. Do you two remember each other from mine and Nessa's engagement do?' Ward gestured behind his shoulder, and she met Crispin's dark, silent gaze as her brother made unnecessary introductions.

'Vaguely.' She prayed he wouldn't contradict her and mention their far more recent confrontation. 'I've heard Nessa singin' your praises and I'm sure she's over the moon you're back. I appreciate you givin' us a hand.'

'No problem.'

'So? Trusted? Not trusted?' Ward grinned.

She reined in her tendency to micro-manage. 'I'm sure you'll be fine. You know the plan. Let me know when you're done and I'll come check it out. Lowena and I are gettin' ready to make one of your old favourites – candy apples – only she calls them toffee apples. Are you a fan, Crispin?'

'Me?' His thick brows shot up. 'I haven't had one since I was a boy. I don't eat sweets much.'

'I'm sure Lowena will force you to sample one. She's a force of nature.'

'I can outlast her.' A shimmer of amusement softened his granite expression. 'I've had plenty of practice at being stubborn.'

'I can believe that.' His swarthy skin turned ruddy under her gaze. 'Anyway, thanks again.' She retreated and closed the door firmly behind her. It disturbed her that Crispin made her heart race in a way no other man had since she'd met Bunny Radnor in a Nashville nightclub on her seventeenth birthday. *Remember how that ended*, she reminded herself.

'What did Ward want?' Lowena bustled in and her sharp blue eyes fixed on Ashley while she gave the briefest possible explanation. 'Crispin's a good man. I used to complain to Nessa that he was a lazy scrounger, but I discovered later how hard-working he really was.' She shook her head. 'He'd had a rough time in the army ... I'm sure he did and saw things most of us wouldn't care to imagine. It's left a mark on him.'

A sliver of guilt lodged in Ashley's stomach for the way she'd reacted when they'd met again last week.

'Anyway, we'd better get busy. We have to do the coating in batches or the toffee will seize up before we've got time to cover the apples.' Lowena bustled over to the range. The old cast iron cooker was a complete mystery to her, but Nessa's sister handled it the same competent way she did everything else. 'I'm going to start by heating this first pan of sugar, lemon juice and water, then when I give you the nod you pass me the golden syrup that's already measured out. Last of all, I'll add the red food colouring.'

Soon a wonderful sweet aroma filled the kitchen, bringing back memories of her mother and grandmother making candy around the holidays.

Hours later they flopped on a couple of chairs and gave each other satisfied high fives. Ashley's back and legs ached from being hunched over for so long while snatching completed apples from Lowena and setting them on the protective paper. The exacting nature of the recipe suited her friend, who'd watched the candy thermometer like a hawk and counted the precise number of drops of food colouring to make sure the apples were uniformly red.

'Knock, knock, we're ready for inspection.' Ward stuck his head around the back door. 'Oh wow, those look amazing!'

'Yeah – they do, don't they?' Ashley couldn't hide her pride at the rows of near-perfect toffee apples. 'I can't wait to see what you've done.'

'Snag us a couple of cold drinks?'

'Will do.' She grabbed two bottles of water from the fridge and swapped out her shoes. 'Are you coming, Lowena?'

'I'll see it later. The kitchen needs cleaning.' That wasn't a complaint or a plea for help, because they all knew she wouldn't trust anyone else to do the job properly.

After being in the warm kitchen all morning, Ashley relished the hint of crispness in the air; every day now the evenings were drawing in earlier. Ashley headed around the corner of the house, a few steps behind Ward, and saw Crispin waiting for them in front of the finished maze. The simple design she'd sketched had turned out well; it was aimed at smaller children and built low enough to be non-threatening.

'Toss us the drinks, Ash. We're dyin' of thirst here.'

She dragged her attention back and passed her brother one bottle then held out the other to Crispin. Ashley couldn't avoid noticing he'd shed the long-sleeved shirt he'd arrived in and his thick, muscular body filled out a faded grey T-shirt in a distracting way.

'Thanks.'

Their fingers intertwined when he reached for the water bottle and, out of the corner of her eye, she caught Ward giving them curious looks. The hint of a smile played around Crispin's mouth as he let go of her hand, popped open the bottle and took a couple of long swallows.

'I'd better get a move on. Nessa's got more work needs doing.' Crispin shrugged in Ward's direction. 'You know what she's like.'

'I sure do. I'm stayin' a while longer. I'll see ya later – and thanks.'

A sliver of satisfaction ran through her when Crispin scarpered as if his tail was on fire.

Chapter Four

'Oh my gosh, that was awesome. I've never had so much fun on Halloween before.' Nessa trotted into the kitchen followed by Ward hauling Tristan in his car seat. 'You should've come.'

Crispin finished tightening the new tap he'd installed while they were out and wiped his hands on a rag. 'I had plenty to keep me busy.'

'And you don't do crowds. We know.' Her gentle teasing didn't bother him. 'What do you think?' She turned her face to show off an exotic red and black snake painted on the curve of her cheek. 'Ashley's so clever. I swear that woman can do anything.'

'It's great. Did a lot of people show up?'

'The place was overrun.' Ward set the baby carrier on the table and wrangled with the straps. Tristan's face got progressively redder and he expelled an ear-splitting yell when his father eventually freed him. 'Damn things. Might as well put a kid in a straightjacket and be done with it.'

'Someone's hungry and ready for a nap.' Nessa swooped in and plucked her son to safety.

'I need to go back and help clear up.' Ward sighed. 'Unless we do it tonight, the local teenagers will take it as an open invitation for mischief.'

'You want a hand?' Crispin felt obliged to offer.

'Sure, that'd be great. You want somethin' to eat first?'

'Nah, I'm good.'

'Lowena will feed you. It's what she does.' Nessa jiggled Tristan to keep his I-want-milk noises to a whimper. 'Don't hurry back. I'll grab a sandwich when this monster drops off and go to bed myself. I'm pooped.' She kissed Ward's cheek and headed for the stairs.

Crispin slipped his camouflage jacket back on. 'We walking up?'

'Nah, let's take the truck so we can bring back the folding tables. Now I've finally bought one, we might as well make good use of it.' He cracked a grin. 'My dear wife thought it was a waste of money. She didn't get that it's every southern man's birth-right to own a pick-up.'

'They're handy.'

'Sure are. C'mon.'

They made their way outside and got in the truck before heading off up the road.

'You settlin' in okay?' Ward slid him a questioning look.

'Yep, pretty good.' He tried to make an effort. 'You must find Cornwall a big change from Tennessee?'

'It sure is. Mostly it's all good, but I miss my folks and decent hamburgers. Y'all serve your beer warm too – I don't reckon I'll ever get used to *that*.'

'Serving it cold kills the taste.' Not that he touched the stuff these days, but the other man knew that. He'd used it as a crutch in his stressful army days before finding healthier ways to cope.

'I guess we'll have to agree to disagree there. What about Wales? Do you miss it?'

'Not really. I left home at sixteen so I haven't lived there in forever.' He'd learned to blank out the homesickness that had gnawed at him as a young squaddie. Occasional visits to his sister, Rhonda, were enough these days.

'Nessa reckons Wales is a bit like Cornwall?' Ward

turned to drive in through the old granite gateposts leading into Tregereth House.

'Parts of the coast are.' A suspicion snaked in that Nessa had put her husband up to these questions. Crispin resented being treated like someone who needed nurturing. He'd looked after himself for twenty-plus years and was doing okay.

Adrenaline fizzed through Ashley's brain. This exultation after today's successful Halloween festival reminded her of being the top scorer on the high school soccer team when they'd won the state championship. She probably wouldn't wind down until about midnight and then she'd crash.

'Next time we must do more apples. We sold out in the first couple of hours.' Lowena glanced up from her list. 'What do you think of extending into the evening? We could have an adult fancy-dress competition? A barbecue and beer tent? Maybe a haunted hay-ride?'

'Next time?' She threw back her head and roared with laughter. 'You know what they'd all say if they heard us now? That we need our heads tested.'

They'd both been astounded by the crowds of people who'd turned up. A decent number were locals, but the selective advertising they'd arranged paid dividends and brought in visitors from all over the county.

Nessa heard the crunch of wheels on the gravel outside and wasn't surprised when her brother opened the back door a minute later and poked his head around.

'How're my clever ladies doin'?'

'Tired.' Lowena's dry comment made him smile. 'If you're looking for dinner, you're out of luck.'

'We came to load up the tables and get them out of your way, and we're happy to do anythin' else you need while we're at it. I've got my trusty helper so you don't have to lift a finger.'

Heat prickled Ashley's neck as she caught a glimpse of Crispin lurking in the shadows.

'Hey, I've got an awesome idea.' Ward's grin widened. 'After we've got the work done, we'll run down to the farm and unload, then come back to pick you both up and we'll grab a bite to eat in the pub.'

'Sounds lovely.' Lowena closed her notebook and slipped her reading glasses back in their neat black leather case.

'I'll text Nessa to make sure she doesn't need me but I should be good. She was planning an early night.' Ward pulled out his phone.

Over his head, Ashley caught Crispin's eye and guessed they were thinking along the same lines. Neither wanted Tristan to be sick, but if her nephew was a bit fractious and fussy that might be enough to nix the dinner plans.

'No problem.' Ward shoved his mobile away again. 'She told us to have a good time. Sooner we get done the sooner we can eat.' He shooed Crispin out.

'What're you wearing?' Lowena's forehead knotted in a frown.

'Wearing? I wasn't planning to change.' Ashley dragged herself up to standing and stretched her arms over her head, swaying from side to side to unravel a few of the kinks. 'Are you gonna wear a ballgown or somethin'?'

'Hardly. But it wouldn't do us any harm to smarten ourselves up a bit.' Her friend's gaze softened.

This was clearly aimed at her because Lowena was her

usual immaculate self. 'Look, I know you mean well, but if I wasn't perfectly made-up with my hair done and smartly dressed ready to cook Bunny's breakfast, I suffered for it. So, if I want to slop around the rest of my life without a scrap of make-up and in old jeans then I will.'

'I'm sorry. I didn't mean to upset you.'

Now *she'd* spoiled a wonderful day. 'No, I'm sorry. I'm tired, that's all.' They both knew that wasn't the whole truth. The question was whether she stuck to her guns out of pure stubbornness or gave in a little?

Crispin hunched further down in the seat when he caught a waft of Ashley's woodsy perfume as she climbed into the truck. He said nothing and kept his attention fixed firmly ahead of him for the short drive back down to Polgarth.

'Right gang, let's celebrate.' Ward parked outside the pub and hopped out.

He ended up last out of the truck, which meant he entered The Chough behind Ashley. Snug brown cord trousers emphasised her petite figure, and when she stopped to slip off a suede jacket the colour of rich honey, the simple cream sweater she wore underneath skimmed her slender curves. The orange plastic pumpkin-shaped lights strung around the bar picked up the shine in her tousled blonde hair.

'What're you drinkin'?' Ward gave his arm a poke.

'Uh, soda and lime. A pint.'

They fetched the drinks and joined the two women at a table to one side of the blazing log fire.

'What's everyone having to eat?' Ward studied the menu.

'What do you reckon to the curry, Crispin? Is it gonna kick my ass?'

'No clue. I haven't eaten here. Never been inside the door.' His mumbled response made Ashley stare.

'Really? I can't get enough of your cute pubs.'

Now he wished he'd kept his mouth shut.

'I'll give the curry a try and hope it doesn't blow my head off.' Ward flashed an easy grin.

'I'll join you, then we can explode together.' Crispin was irrationally pleased when Ashley's mouth lifted at the edges.

'You can order me the steak and mushroom pie.' Lowena gave a small shrug. 'No doubt I could sue Benjy Martin under the Trade Description Act for calling it homemade, but I won't quibble tonight.'

'That makes a change.' Ashley scoffed. 'I thought I was fussy until I met you.'

'You are. We fuss about different things, that's all.'

Their disagreement disturbed him for a second, until he realised that the two women were joking with each other.

'Ash?' Ward waved a menu at her. 'Is it a salmon and mixed salad with no dressing night, or are you going for a pasty after all of today's hard work?'

A mottled flush crept up her neck. Crispin was puzzled by her reaction for a moment, but then remembered Polly confiding in him once that Ashley had lingering food issues thanks to her controlling ex-husband.

'You could throw your hat in with us and risk the curry?' Crispin's quick suggestion made her wide hazel eyes brim over with gratitude.

'Yeah, why not?'

The relief in Ashley's voice combined with her warm smile sent a wave of panic rolling through him *Oh God, was he ever in trouble now?* he thought. One reason army life ate him up and spat him out in the end was because he couldn't resist trying to be, as his last commander put it, "Everyone's fuckin' white knight". He even rescued spiders and carried them somewhere safe rather than squash them under his size twelve boots. His automatic kindness to Ashley had started from that same innate urge, but there was nothing run of the mill about the tug of physical attraction he experienced every time in her presence. That scared him.

'Don't bother ordering for me. I've changed my mind about the curry.' He pushed his chair back, scraping the legs over the slate tiles. 'I'm not really that hungry and I've got an early start in the morning.' That was complete bull. He hadn't eaten since breakfast so there was a hole where his stomach used to be, plus Nessa wouldn't bang on his door at the crack of dawn demanding he get to work. He steeled himself to ignore the three shocked stares aimed in his direction and stalked out.

Back in the crisp night air, his jangled nerves settled and he stepped aside to let a noisy, laughing group of young people in Halloween costumes enter the pub. Crispin couldn't remember ever being that carefree.

He stuck his hands in his pockets and marched off down the road, not looking back.

Chapter Five

Tristan's soft downy head bobbled off of Ashley's shoulder and she inhaled his sweet baby scent. All week she'd been out of sorts since Crispin's abrupt departure from the pub on Halloween night. One minute they were laughing together, and he'd been kindness itself when Ward blundered over her food choices, but then it was as if someone flicked a switch and everything changed. Deep down she suspected he was as freaked out as she was by the undeniable pull of desire fizzling between them every time they were around each other.

'Do you want another coffee?' Polly tapped on the table in front of her.

'Uh, sorry … I was miles away.' She stared at her empty cup. 'Yeah, that'd be great.'

'I'll fetch it on the condition you pass Tris over in return.'

'I love that he's become the communal Pear Tree Farm baby.' Nessa smiled. 'He has no idea how lucky he is, but *I* know I couldn't do it without you all. Ward is an incredible dad but we've got two businesses to run, and no one warns you how much time babies take up.'

'If they did, the human race would die out.' Lowena slapped a hand over her mouth. 'Oh God. I'm sorry, Polly.'

Because the subject was taboo in everyday conversation, Ashley often forgot the story Ward shared with her once about Polly and Jack. As young parents they lost their baby son in a house fire in Birmingham, and to escape the scene of the tragedy and the condemnation of their families, that's when they'd set off in their pink VW camper and ended up settling in Cornwall.

'It's all right.'

'No, it isn't.' Lowena sounded distraught.

'Oh, love. You didn't say it on purpose to hurt me. Let's forget it.' Polly tried to brush it off. 'I thought you got us here to talk about some sort of Christmas festival?'

'We won't have long before a certain little boy will be screaming to be fed again.' Nessa's rueful smile defused the awkward moment. 'Plus, *someone* has her weekly appointment to get the latest outrageous hairstyle.'

'And we've still got to make treats for y'all's Bonfire Night thing tonight.' Ashley chimed back in. The plan was to watch Polgarth's fifth of November fireworks together from the farm's upper field.

'You're right, let's get on with business.' Lowena pulled out her thick black leather binder. 'Now, Nessa, hear us out properly before you tell us what you think. We know your in-laws are coming and you've got Tris to care for. We're not expecting you to do any extra work.'

'Coffee.' Polly set a steaming mug in front of Ashley and held out her arms. 'We had a deal.'

Everyone laughed as she huffed an exaggerated sigh and handed him over.

'I know we're a bit late in the year coming up with this,' Lowena continued, 'but I think we can pull it off. Another year we—'

'Oh God, I don't even want to know what you might dream up *next* year.' Nessa's eyebrows shot skywards.

'If you keep interrupting, we'll never get anything

settled.' Lowena glared at her sister. 'We can cope with the extra workload – can't we, Ashley?'

'No problem. Assuming we can talk Ward around.'

'He doesn't know?' Nessa looked perturbed.

'Not yet, but if we present a united front he's bound to agree.' Lowena's blithe assumption made everyone smile. 'Ashley came up with the concept in the first place and we've got an initial plan sorted out already. We're calling the festival "Christmas, Cornish Style" and thinking of holding it on the three weekends leading up to Christmas, so it'll all be over before the actual holiday. We'll have events here at the farm and up at Tregereth with Cornish themed food, local festive crafts and live music.'

'It sounds wonderful … but aren't all the decent musicians and crafters booked by now?' Polly sounded dubious.

'Not necessarily.' The colour rose in Lowena's face. 'I've already put out a few feelers and got several pencilled in. And I checked with the vicar and the parish council to make sure we won't clash with any other Christmas festivities. You know, the church itself is closed for repairs to the roof and they're using the hall next door for everything? They've got several crafters in the congregation, so I thought we could offer them a couple of free stalls. Let them keep the money they raise for the roof fund and we could donate a percentage of our overall profits too.'

'That's a generous idea. I like that!' Nessa gave a helpless shrug. 'I suppose we can give it a try.'

'Wonderful. I knew you'd love it.'

A flutter of excitement lodged in Ashley's stomach. If the festival was a success, it should help prove to her parents that she was carving out a successful life here.

'Will you broach the subject with Ward, or do you want us to?' Lowena asked.

'I'll do it. Tonight.'

'Dig out your sexy lingerie and black stockings and he'll be putty in your hands.'

'For heaven's sake. I don't have to resort to that sort of thing. We'll talk it over in a perfectly adult fashion.'

'Spoilsport.' Ward's deep voice rumbled from the doorway. 'I came in on the end of the conversation so I've no idea what the Polgarth coven are conspiring about now, but I'm with Lowena on this one.' Her brother's wicked gaze dragged over his wife. 'I'm shallow.'

'You're all terrible and embarrassing.' She snatched Tristan away from Polly. 'I refuse to have my innocent baby corrupted any longer around you lot.' Nessa barged past Ward and he raced after her, pleading and begging her to listen to him.

The three of them left behind burst out laughing.

'I know you're not much for fireworks – had enough of the real thing in the army, I suppose – but at least come down and eat with us before they start,' Polly pleaded. 'Ward's grilling some proper American burgers.'

Crispin had made a promise with himself when he returned to be more sociable, but between trying to avoid Ashley and his naturally solitary nature, it was proving a challenge. His old friend was spot on about his dislike of unexpected loud noises – these days he associated them with disaster rather than entertainment.

'Lowena's making parkin.'

'You've found my weakness there. My mum always made it on Bonfire Night.' He rarely ate any sort of sweets, but thinking about the spicy, sticky cake made his mouth water. 'I'll be there.'

'We're starting about six o'clock. Up near the shepherd's huts.' Polly looked triumphant.

'Should I make a miniature Guy Fawkes to stick on your head?' He carefully patted her tower of bright red and orange curls.

'You're a cheeky boy.' She giggled and ran off.

Crispin ambled back to his caravan and kicked off his muddy work boots. After a cup of tea and a hot shower to slough off the evidence of his day spent in the garden, he pulled out his razor to do battle with almost two weeks' worth of thick stubble. He hated to go empty-handed and grabbed a six pack of Coke from the fridge before he tugged his boots back on.

His nerves flared when he spotted his friends gathered around a small fire blazing in an empty oil drum. Over to one side he saw Ward hunched over a smoking grill.

'Don't even think about it.' Ashley's soft drawl warmed the back of his neck. A drift of her perfume sneaked up too, reminding Crispin of ripe oranges with a punch of spice thrown in.

'About what?' He swung around and felt his cheeks heat when her sparkling hazel eyes zeroed in on him. She knew he'd been on the point of legging it.

'Leaving. I've heard there's a big slice of that parkin stuff with your name on it.'

Crispin trudged along next to her and they joined the rest of the group.

'You owe me a pound.' Polly snickered and prodded her long-suffering husband in the ribs.

'I'm glad you didn't risk all of your fortune, Jack.' Crispin managed to make a joke of it.

'I did, mate, but there's a chance if you bugger off now she might let me keep my money.'

'Tough luck. I'm staying.' He dredged up a smile.

'The burgers are ready,' Ward yelled over. 'Come and get 'em.'

'Let's go – and I'll take one of those too, unless they're all for you?' Ashley pointed to the cans of drink he'd forgotten he was carrying.

'Uh no, of course they aren't. I brought them to share.'

'Hey Crispin, I bet you could murder one of these? Ward waved a spatula at the sizzling burgers. 'Or two?'

'One's fine, thanks.'

'Ash will show you the fixin's.' He passed them each a loaded paper plate.

Before he had the chance to say he was happy to eat it plain, Crispin found himself steered over to a small table where Ashley grabbed his plate and rattled off all the additions she planned to make unless he told her otherwise. Less than a minute later she passed it back, doubled in size now thanks to the bacon, cheese, lettuce, tomato, pickles, mustard and ketchup she'd loaded on.

'Let's go join the others. Lowena insisted we set up a table and chairs because she refused to stand around a muddy field eating a burger in her hands, even for us – her words exactly.' Her husky laughter broke out. 'She was all set to bring knives and forks for everyone until Ward half-jokingly threatened to fire her if she did.'

'I've spent years eating anything, anywhere, in all kinds

of conditions.' Crispin gazed around them. 'This is luxury, trust me.'

Ashley gave him a lingering look but said nothing. Bad experiences made a person wary and she'd clearly had her fill of them too. He guessed that, like him, she'd worked hard to reach a place of relative contentment. She didn't need him rocking her fragile boat any more than he needed her unsettling his.

'If we let our burgers get cold, Ward'll string us up.' He didn't miss the pleading edge to her voice, urging him to play along.

'That'd be a shame. I wouldn't get any of your delicious parkin then.'

'It might be lousy for all you know.'

'No way. Lowena made it, so it's bound to be perfect.' His casual response made the shadows fall away from Ashley's strained face, leaving behind her gentle smile. That made him feel ten feet tall. Good news? Bad news? That was debatable.

Chapter Six

'Can you believe that's the second lot I've had to turn down?' Lowena marched into the kitchen brandishing her mobile. 'We're fully booked here for all three of the Christmas festival weekends.'

'That's awesome.' Ashley was pleased and relieved that the hard work they'd put in over the last couple of weeks was paying off. Ever since the Bonfire Night party, when she and Crispin nibbled around the edges of flirting with each other, she'd dumped all of her excess energy into organising the "Christmas, Cornish Style" event.

'Oh, by the way, did I remember to mention you're going to be interviewed about the festival on Radio Cornwall on Wednesday afternoon?'

'What? You *know* you didn't.' The accusation brought out her friend's smug smile. 'No way. No. You'll have to do it.'

'Don't be silly. A real live American will be far more interesting to the listeners.'

'You can send Ward instead.'

Lowena shook her head. 'You know I love your dear brother, but this isn't his thing.'

'It's not mine either, I—'

'I've already sent Hilary Parnell all the details, and she's great at her job. She'll put you at your ease and ask the right questions.' She gathered up a duster and tin of spray polish. 'If you need me, I'll be doing the bedrooms. Why don't you work on the list of prospective food providers and ring up the ones I haven't been able to get hold of yet?'

Ashley gave up. 'Fine. Where's the list?'

'It's … oh damn.' Lowena looked contrite. 'Sorry. It's not like me to be careless, but I left the folder with Nessa yesterday evening when I was going over more ideas with her and Polly. If you walk down to pick it up, they might take pity and offer to give you a hand. They know a lot of people on the list.'

'Is it raining?'

'Not yet – but a bit of rain won't kill you! If you plan on staying in Cornwall long-term, you might as well get used to it.' Lowena breezed off, and Ashley couldn't resist sticking out her tongue at her friend's retreating back.

Ward had adapted faster than her to the generally mild, damp climate and relished striding around in muddy wellington boots and wearing one of the ubiquitous green waxed coats. She sighed and fetched the bright red mac she'd bought after being soaked to the skin one too many times.

Ashley had only taken a couple of steps outside the back door when drops of rain started to plop out of the grey, stormy sky. She tugged up her hood as Mother Nature proceeded to test her by turning it up a few notches and unleashing a proper downpour. After scurrying down the road, she ducked under the narrow porch jutting out over Nessa's front door and struggled to unlace her shoes.

'Need a hand?' Crispin suddenly appeared out of the gloom.

'I'm tryin' to get these off, but my fingers are numb with the cold. I should've worn gloves.'

'You need wellies too.' He smirked at her impractical trainers. 'Got to get with the programme.'

'Oh God, if another person tells me that I'll scream. I know, all right?' Ashley heaved a sigh. 'Sorry, this lousy weather isn't your fault.'

'You don't appreciate the glorious Cornish climate?'

'I'm workin' on it.'

He crouched down and unknotted her laces. It caught her unawares when he wrapped one strong hand around her ankle and lifted her foot up to prise off the shoe then went through the same ritual with the other one.

'Does that mean you're planning to stay?' His intense gaze made her stomach fizz. 'I hope so.'

'Do you?'

'Yes, why wouldn't I?' Crispin tugged off his boots and set them next to her shoes on the mat before pulling off his waterproof cape and hanging it on one of iron pegs jutting out of the bricks.

I suspect that's a question for another day, she thought. She breezed in past him without answering and found her sister-in-law in the kitchen walking a fretful Tristan around. 'Hiya, how's our baby today?'

'Refusing to take a nap.'

'Are you all right?' Ashley noticed her sister-in-law's normal ready smile was nowhere in sight and her eyes were red-rimmed with tiredness. 'Did you get much sleep last night?'

'Not really – and before you say anything, Ward would've helped but he doesn't have boobs.'

'Uh, shall I come back later?' Crispin hovered in the doorway. 'I only came down to see if you'd heard whether the new polytunnel is in yet?'

'Yes, it is but—'

'You can sort that out later.' Ashley cut off the conversation. 'Has Tristan been fed recently, Nessa?'

'Yes, why?'

'What about you? Have you eaten this morning?'

'Only a cup of tea.' Nessa looked wary. 'And don't blame Ward for that either. I insisted he went off to meet with the Wheal Boys as planned to run through a couple of new songs he's written. They're planning to sing them on Christmas Eve down at the pub.'

She'd have a quiet word with her brother later. Or a not so quiet one. '*You* are going upstairs right now and getting back into bed. I'll rustle up some breakfast and, after you've eaten every last scrap, you're gonna take a good long nap.'

'But I need to get Tristan to sleep first.'

'Give him to Crispin.' Ashley threw him a look she hoped conveyed the message – *don't let me down.*

'Oh yeah, sure. No problem.'

Nessa looked uncertain as she passed over the grizzling little boy, and Crispin handled Tristan as if he was an unexploded bomb that might detonate at any second.

'Now shoo.' Ashley waved her away. 'I'll be up with your food soon.'

'You're wonderful. You both are.' She scurried out of the kitchen, as though if she dawdled they might change their minds.

'Why didn't we see she was struggling?'

'Don't beat yourself up. We'll help now.' Crispin's reassuring words calmed her down. 'If you prefer it, I'll cook and you can babysit?'

Ashley laughed at his obvious attempt to swap roles. 'It's okay. I'm good. You baby whisperer. Me bacon fryer.'

Crispin hated the idea of letting her down but fully expected Tristan to start wailing at being held by someone who had no clue what they were doing. Instead, the baby's big blue eyes popped open and studied him for a few seconds before his thick dark lashes fluttered closed.

'Wow, you've got the magic touch.'

'Flattery will get you everywhere.'

'I thought it might.' Ashley's artless grin stirred him. 'I'd better hurry with this breakfast or Nessa will be fast asleep.'

He retreated to the old rocking chair in the corner and shifted the little boy up against his chest. Ward had dug the chair out of the attic at Tregereth House and repaired it ready for the baby's arrival. He'd glued a wobbly arm back together before spending hours sandpapering it, then repainting the wood a soft moss-green to match the kitchen.

'They should bottle this fragrance. There's nothin' like the smell of bacon frying,' Ashley commented as she chopped a pile of mushrooms to add to the sizzling pan.

'I'm not going to disagree there.'

Ashley set a tray on the table and started to load it up. 'Nessa will gripe about the decaf coffee but regular will keep her awake. That's everything, I think. I won't be long.'

'We'll be fine.' Left alone with the sleeping baby, he crooned a Welsh lullaby. He didn't notice Ashley return.

'Wow, Nessa was right. She said you had an awesome voice.' She gazed at him from the doorway and Crispin felt a rush of heat zoom up his neck. 'How many other secrets do you have?'

'Come and have a drink with me tonight and I might tell you some of them.' The rash offer popped out before he stopped to think what he was saying. 'I mean—'

'I'd love to.'

'Really?'

'Unless you've changed your mind already?' The gleam in her eyes grew brighter. She craned her neck to peer out of the window as a vehicle crunched on the gravel outside. 'It's Ward. Will you be okay if I nab him? My brother needs to hear a few home truths without Nessa around being all British and nice.'

'No problem.' Crispin was left wondering about that evening. Had he just made another mistake?

Chapter Seven

'Oh … hi, Ash. I didn't know you were comin' down today?' Ward grabbed his laptop bag off the back seat and stepped across to give her a hug.

'You should be glad I did.'

'What's wrong? Is Tris all right? Nessa?' Panic shot through his voice.

'Yeah, they're fine – but we need to talk.'

'Okay.' Her brother looked wary. 'Can we get in out of the rain first?'

'Yeah, but not in the kitchen. Crispin's in there rocking Tris.'

'Why on earth—'

'And Nessa's taking a nap, so you need to keep your voice down.' She was relieved when he didn't ask any further questions until they were settled in the dining room with the door closed. The story tumbled out of her.

'Why didn't she say?' Ward's voice thickened with emotion. 'I've pleaded with her to pump or use formula occasionally so I could feed Tris and give her a break … but she's stubborn.'

'Well, *you'll* have to be more stubborn. I wouldn't normally interfere between the two of you, but I didn't feel I had a choice this time.'

'Yeah, I know – and thanks.' He dredged up a faint smile. 'Don't expect Nessa to thank you for a while though.'

'I can live with that.' Last year the shoe had been on the other foot. She hadn't appreciated her brother's interference until the whole sorry episode with her now ex-husband was over and she could breathe freely again. 'What I really came down for was the list of possible food vendors, so I'd better dig up that and disappear – it's probably best I'm not around when Nessa wakes up. I'll let Crispin know I'm off.' Ashley wasn't stupid enough to mention their potential plans for that evening – it would no doubt result in unwanted brotherly advice.

If anything melted a woman's heart faster than seeing a rugged man cradling a sleeping baby, she couldn't imagine what it might be. The sight of Crispin's broad, weather-beaten hands cradling Tristan brought a lump to her throat.

'You spying on me?'

'Of course not.' Ashley glanced around the room. 'There's the list I came for.' She grabbed a folder off the counter. 'If you don't mind, I'm clearin' off while the goin's good.'

'No probs. Me and Tris are fine.' He stroked the little boy's back. 'You run on.' Crispin raised one dark eyebrow. 'Tonight? Seven o'clock? I'll cook dinner if you like.'

'Can I bring anything?'

'Just you.' His gravelly whisper kicked the pull of desire between them up another level.

'I can manage that.'

The hint of a smile pulled at his mouth, and the good intentions she'd made to keep him at arm's length spiralled well and truly out of reach.

'Been doing a bit of shopping?' Polly scurried out from the camp site's laundry room, and Crispin took an educated guess she'd been watching out of the window in case she missed anything that might be going on.

'Yep.' He tightened his grip on the two bags of groceries he'd carried back from the village.

'I hear you helped poor Nessa out earlier. Good for you. I've been telling that girl for weeks she needed to take better care of herself.' She was clearly fishing for more information but he'd no intention of obliging.

'I'd better get on before my ice cream melts.'

'I thought you never ate much sweet stuff?'

Lying was pointless when they lived so close that Polly was bound to see his visitor arrive. 'I'm cooking dinner for a friend.'

'That's a first. Ashley, is it?' She smirked when he didn't reply. 'Have you got enough dishes and cutlery? I can lend you anything if—'

'I'm fine – but thanks for offering. Better go.'

'What're you making?'

'Food.' He tossed the word back over his shoulder and strode away.

Once he had the jacket potatoes in the oven alongside a chicken and mushroom casserole, Crispin hurried to get dressed. He deliberated between the only three half-decent shirts he owned and settled on a dark blue one along with his least-worn pair of jeans. He dragged a comb through his thick hair, then shaved and rubbed his hand over his face to check for any spots he'd missed. *God, I'm acting worse than a love-sick teenage boy*, he thought.

Crispin tried to see the caravan through Ashley's eyes before telling himself not to be stupid. This was no blind date. A light tap on the door sent him rushing to answer it.

'Do I have spinach between my teeth?' She hovered on the top step with the wind catching her blonde hair.

'Why? Were you eating some?'

'No, but you're staring.'

'Sorry.' If he admitted that her natural beauty bowled him over every time they met, she'd give one of the husky laughs that tied him in knots.

'Uh ... is there any chance you might invite me in?'

'Sorry. Again.' A waft of sultry perfume teased him as she brushed past. 'I'd show you around the caravan, but you've seen them all before so—'

'Crispin, this is me.' Out of nowhere, she wrapped her slender arms around his neck and planted a brief decisive kiss on his mouth before letting go with a satisfied smile. 'There. That gets that out of the way.'

'Out of the way?'

Two circles of heat bloomed in her cheeks. 'That's not how I meant to phrase it. I've wondered what kissing you would be like, and I suspect you've done the same about me ... at least I hope so.'

'Yes. Oh yes.' His fervent response made her face light up.

'Awesome. I hoped if I took the initiative, you wouldn't have to wonder if it's okay to kiss me later.'

'You wouldn't want another?'

'Oh God ... I think we need to start this conversation over.'

'I hate saying sorry again, but I'm out of practice with this ... flirting ... women.'

'I'm glad. Look, you invited me for a meal and to talk – and I'm guessing we both need friendship as much as anythin' else.' Shyness threaded through her voice. 'It doesn't have to rule out more kisses though.'

42

He hadn't been standing close enough before to notice the dusting of freckles on her flawless skin. 'Now or later?'

'Does it have to be either/or?'

Crispin took that as an offer and lowered his mouth to brush against hers. He lost the battle to keep things light when her tongue flicked against his lip. The lingering kiss acted like a drug on his senses and, when he slid his hands around her waist to tug her closer, her glazed eyes struggled to focus on him.

'Is something burning?' Ashley pulled back and sniffed at the air.

The tempting smell of fragrant herbs and succulent chicken had been replaced by acrid fumes. Black smoke poured out of the oven and then the smoke detector started to wail. Crispin put his brain in gear and grabbed a cloth to pull the casserole out and set it on top of the hob before he turned off the alarm. Next, he retrieved the charred remains of the jacket potatoes. 'Open the door. I'll get the windows.' In a couple of minutes, his eyes stopped stinging and the air began to clear.

'What was it?' She peered over his shoulder as he lifted the lid.

'Chicken casserole.' The dried up remains mocked him. He couldn't understand what had happened until he glanced at the temperature dial. 'Damn. I set it too high. Must've been distracted.'

'Can't imagine why.'

'Me neither.'

Ashley giggled and covered her mouth with her hand. 'I'm sorry, it's not funny really.'

'Yep, it is.' His rueful smile set her off laughing again. 'It's typical of my luck. For the first time in years, I attempt to romance a woman and almost end up calling the fire brigade.'

'Is everything all right?' Jack's anxious face appeared at the door. 'We saw smoke and heard your alarm.'

'Oh, good grief. What've you done, my love?' Polly leaned in too.

'I burned our dinner.'

Ashley linked her arm through his. 'It's fine. We'll get it sorted.'

'We'll leave you to it.' Jack prodded his wife's arm. 'Let's go back to ours. They don't need us bothering them.'

'You weren't bothering us.' Crispin hated the thought of offending them. 'I appreciate you coming over to check.' He caught Jack suppressing a smile. They both knew of Polly's tendency towards well-intentioned nosiness. 'Goodnight.'

On their own again, he sighed as he looked at Ashley. 'What now?'

'Well, for a start it's freezing.' She couldn't help shivering as a blast of cold air shot through the caravan. 'I borrowed Lowena's car to drive down, so I didn't bother with a coat – and this blouse is thin.'

'If you're happy to stay here, I can lend you a thick jumper … or we could go somewhere else. The pub maybe?'

'Make me a mug of hot coffee and I'll be good.'

'One jumper coming up.'

Ashley smiled to herself when he disappeared down the narrow hallway. She'd talked herself in and out of coming here tonight a million times, and if it hadn't been for

Lowena, she might not be here now. Her friend had told her to give Crispin a chance. And herself.

She filled up the kettle and took two mugs out of a neat, well-organised cupboard then found the instant coffee.

'Here you go.' Crispin offered her a chunky grey jumper that'd seen better days.

They both laughed when she tugged it on because it almost reached her knees and made her look like a little girl playing dress-up. Ashley had to fold back the sleeves multiple times to re-discover her fingers.

'Why don't you go and sit on the sofa? There're a couple of blankets you can wrap up in and I'll turn on the electric fire. I'll stick the burned dish and the potatoes outside but I don't want to close the caravan up just yet.'

A few minutes later he joined her, carrying two steaming mugs of coffee and a plate of hot, buttered toast. 'I hope this will do. I didn't find anything else I could fix in a hurry.'

'It'll do fine. Now I want to know everything about you.'

'Could be a long night.' His rich Welsh accent thickened.

'I've nowhere to be.' The simple, disingenuous answer made his deep hooded eyes turn pitch-black.

Crispin settled down by her and tucked a thick green plaid blanket in around them. She didn't rush to fill the silence and eventually he heaved a sigh.

'Growing up we struggled a bit because my dad died when I was small. Mam did her best but I always remember the Christmas I was eight years old when I couldn't understand why I received a patched up second-hand bike for Christmas instead of a shiny new red one like my best friend. I wasn't much for school apart from any sort of sports and the choir.' He shrugged. 'I failed most of my exams and left soon as I could. There weren't any jobs around our way, and my family weren't happy when I joined the army but they didn't try to stop me.'

'As stubborn as you are, they wouldn't have got far.' Her dry comment dragged a half-smile out of him. 'What did you like about the military life?'

'The comradeship. Sense of purpose. Trying to make a difference in tough places.' He picked up one of her hands and idly stroked it. 'Over time though I started to feel that things would go back to the way they were when we left, and all those good men and women we lost had died in vain.'

'I bet some of the local people would disagree.'

'I suppose the girls and women in particular might, but is it better to taste freedom and then lose it than never know any different?'

'I think you know the answer to that.'

'Maybe. I let it all get to me at the time and started drinking too much. Got in some disciplinary trouble. Didn't exactly disobey orders but skirted pretty close.' A flush tinged his cheeks. 'Then I got involved with a woman I shouldn't have and got sent back to the UK. That hacked me off. I'd had enough of everything at that point and that's when I took off and went AWOL.' His voice turned gruff. 'I should've handled it better and applied to get out officially, but at the time I was desperate.' His granite expression softened. 'I set off walking and ended up in Cornwall.'

Did she want to know more about the woman who'd tipped him over the edge or not? Ashley couldn't decide.

'You know the rest. I turned up here and Nessa took me in. Saved me.' The edge to his voice said not to ask any more. Not now. 'Your turn.'

She hitched a breath and tried to smile. 'You might regret asking.' Before she could lose the courage, Ashley told him about Bunny. Not everything because it was too soon for that but enough for him to hopefully understand her better.

'He didn't deserve you.'

Emotion swelled in her throat and a wave of tiredness swept through her as she nestled against his shoulder.

'It's getting late. Stay.'

'No, I couldn't. It—'

'I didn't mean .... not that I wouldn't ... you can sleep in the spare room.'

Something unspoken hovered in the air between them and Ashley wished she could reassure him that he wasn't the only one with conflicted feelings.

'That sounds great.'

'It might stir up gossip.' His good-humoured warning made her laugh.

'I don't care if you don't?'

He tightened his arms around her and dropped a soft kiss on her forehead. 'Polly needs something else to talk about.'

Chapter Eight

Crispin stirred and checked the time on his bedside clock. It was only five o'clock and still dark outside, but he wouldn't get any more sleep now. He dragged on last night's clothes, then eased the door open and padded along the hall in his bare feet. The lingering scent of smoke still hung around but he'd open up all the windows later.

'Is it all right if I use your bathroom?'

He struggled not to gawk at Ashley. Judging by his tempting view of her bare legs, she'd slept in his baggy jumper and little else.

'Of course. I didn't hear you get up. I'm just going to put the kettle on.'

Crispin made tea for himself and handed her a mug of coffee when she returned. 'Toast?'

'Why not? That seems to be our go-to meal.'

Even the smudges of make-up and lingering hints of tiredness around her eyes couldn't detract from her innate beauty, and when she wandered over to the sofa and tucked her legs up under her to expose several more inches of smooth skin, he considered sticking his head under the cold tap. Instead, he focused on preparing the toast.

'Here we go.'

'Thanks.' Ashley threw him a worried look. 'I hope you don't regret our chat last night?'

'Why would I?'

'Because you're like me ... a private person, most of the time.'

Crispin didn't know the full extent of her ex-husband's

behaviour, but it wasn't hard to fill in the gaps between what she'd told him and what he already knew to form a picture of Bunny Radnor that left a nasty taste in his mouth.

'I hope it means we trust each other. I've never said much to anyone here about my time in the army.' Some stories were still buried so deep, he couldn't imagine letting them out.

'I reckon we're gettin' pretty good at this friend thing. What do you think?'

The answer he knew he should give stuck in his throat. Ashley had stirred longings he thought he'd learned to live without.

'Hey, I liked the other part too.' She nuzzled a kiss on his stubbly cheek. 'In case you weren't sure, it took all my self-restraint to walk away after you kissed me goodnight.'

'Maybe next time you won't be so well disciplined.' That slipped out before he could clamp his mouth shut. 'Sorry. I shouldn't have said that, but—'

'Don't apologise.' Fire swept up her neck. 'I need us to be honest. Bunny ridiculed my opinions to the point that I didn't dare to voice them.' She cleared her throat. 'I'm still working on expressing myself better.' Her smile turned wicked. 'Lowena's a huge help. She's unflinching.'

'She certainly is. I'm not sure I want you to turn quite that ...'

'Frank? Yeah, we'll go with that.' Ashley checked the time on her phone. 'I'm afraid I should get goin'.'

Crispin struggled over what to say. At the end of the day, what did he have to offer this smart, beautiful woman? Everything he owned fitted in this small caravan with space left over. His monthly pay cheque covered his simple needs but his savings were almost non-existent. The bus was his regular mode of transport and his phone was an old school pay-as-you-go type. He was a realist and had stopped believing in miracles a long time ago.

Ashley couldn't help recognising the irony as she watched indecision play across his face. He had no more confidence than she did – possibly less. Many of the stories Crispin shared last night brought her to the verge of tears. The hard, often ugly reality of a life she knew nothing about had shaped him into the man standing in front of her now. Did it make him an unwise choice? Possibly, but her heart was refusing to listen.

'We can play this by ear, can't we? If I ask for more than you're able to give, you can just tell me.' Ashley managed a tiny smile. 'I'll do the same.' His wistful expression said she was so far beyond his reach he didn't stand a chance. When they were at the pub, she'd caught several women sneaking admiring glances his way. Even this morning, with his thick dark hair tangled from sleep, those deep hooded eyes bloodshot from tiredness and his standard stubbly jaw, he still stirred her. 'Does that sound fair to you?'

'Not sure what I'm saying yes to, but I can't seem to say no to you.'

'Awesome. In that case you can kiss me.'

'Oh … can I?' His broad hands slid around her waist. 'Is this what you had in mind?'

He cradled the back of her head with one hand and his strong fingers twined in her hair, making long-neglected parts of her body flutter back to life as he dragged them into a deep, sensual kiss. A satisfied growl rumbled from his throat as he broke away. 'Well?'

'Not bad.' Ashley's admission made him smile.

'Not bad?'

'If I award you ten out of ten, you'll have no room for improvement – and I'm pretty sure being naked in bed would top that.' She couldn't believe she'd said that and blushed.

'You're not having any problem expressing your opinions now.' His eyebrows shot up. 'You don't need bloody Lowena giving you lessons.'

'Are you complainin'?'

'No! I'd rather know where I stand. I haven't been seriously involved with anyone for several years, and we both ended up hurt because we weren't honest about what we wanted from each other.'

'You'll have to tell me more another day.' She rested her hand on his arm. 'I'm real sorry, but I need to get back to Tregereth. I've a ton of work to get on with, and Lowena's lined up an interview for me on Radio Cornwall on Wednesday afternoon to promote the "Christmas, Cornish Style" event so I need to get my ducks in a row if I'm not goin' to come across as an idiot.'

'You'll ace it. I'll make sure to listen in.'

'Oh God, please don't!' Ashley grimaced. 'The thought of people I know hearing me brings me out in a cold sweat.'

'You'll bring the crowds in.' He rolled his thick shoulders in a shrug. 'Don't worry about the other thing; it's not important.'

It mattered very much to her but would have to wait for now. 'I'll call you later.'

Crispin nodded but said nothing as she slung her black messenger bag across her body and left. Outside, she took several deep breaths of the fresh, clean air to clear her head, then strode off down the path.

Crispin only had a towel wrapped around him when there was a knock on the door. After Ashley had left, he'd jumped in the shower. He found Ward standing on the steps.

'Come in. Just let me throw some clothes on, then we'll talk. Do you fancy a cuppa?'

'Nah, I'm good.'

Crispin dressed quickly and raked a comb through his hair before he hurried back out. 'How's Nessa doing, by the way?'

'Much better.' Ward stretched out on the sofa and yawned. 'I'm knackered but that's okay. I'd been an ostrich and my good 'ole sister yanked my head out the sand. She's the best.'

He felt the heat rise in his face thinking about Ashley.

'We've decided to share Tris's feedings now … with a bottle, in case you were wonderin'.' Ward flashed a broad grin.

'I'm relieved to hear it.' Crispin straddled one of the kitchen chairs. 'It's a tough time. Lot of adjustments to make. I'm happy to do anything I can to help. Was there something specific you wanted now?'

'Yeah, I wondered if you're up for takin' on more work? With a pay increase, of course. For a start I'd appreciate you takin' the lead on this Christmas project instead of me.' Ward held up a warning hand. 'Yeah, I know you're not a style guru – you and me both. I'm talkin' about on the logistics side. Ashley, Lowena and Nessa are putting the whole thing together. You'll be the …'

'Brawn?'

'Yeah, pretty much. It'll free me up to take care of other stuff.' He slid Crispin a sideways glance. 'Are you okay? You look a bit down in the mouth. I don't blab, if that's what's worrying you.'

He could hardly talk through his conflicting feelings about Ashley with her protective older brother. 'I didn't get much sleep last night, that's all.'

Ward hauled himself off the sofa. 'We'll have a meeting at our place on Wednesday evening. Come down around six and eat with us. After we get Tristan settled, we'll sort out who's doin' what.'

This would force him into Ashley's proximity more, and he wasn't sure if that was a good or bad thing yet. He guessed they'd find out soon enough.

Chapter Nine

The last time Ashley had experienced this level of nerves was on her wedding day – not a good omen. She carefully squeezed Lowena's car into the last available parking space next to the radio station.

A beep alerted her to a text message from Crispin.

Good luck. Knock 'em dead.

She sent back a smile emoji before shutting off her phone. The last thing she needed was to have it jangling to life in the middle of her interview. As soon as she stepped inside the lobby, a skinny young woman with spiky red hair and a toothy smile appeared.

'Ms Spencer? I'm Mara. We'll go on through to the waiting room. Hilary will be ready for you in a few minutes.'

Ashley clutched her folder of information in one hand and wriggled out of her raincoat as they walked.

'Hilary told me you're American. That's cool.'

She thanked the other woman because she couldn't think of a smart answer that wasn't rude.

The studio was visible through the soundproof glass wall and she recognised the announcer from her picture on the station's website: a plump middle-aged woman with dyed blonde hair and rectangular blue-framed glasses. There were speakers in the waiting room, and she heard Hilary wrapping up an interview with a man about next week's "Festival of Lights" when the city's Christmas lights would be turned on. Ashley ticked one worry off her mental list – she could understand Hilary's soft Cornish accent. As the man left and a carol started to play, Hilary slipped off her headphones and beckoned them in.

The next ten minutes disappeared in a blur. Ashley was introduced as a charming American who'd made Cornwall her home and was now one of the organisers of a new Christmas event. She'd been lulled into forgetting there were thousands of listeners tuning in, and if someone were to put her on the spot, she realised she wouldn't be able to repeat anything she'd just said.

A jolt of satisfaction shot through her. Other people might not consider the interview to be a big deal but to her it was a huge turning point. Her ex-husband put her down for so long that she'd lost sight of what she was capable of. She couldn't wipe the smile from her face as she jumped in the car, pulled back out on the street and then navigated the tricky roundabout in front of her like a local.

She checked the time and decided to head straight for Pear Tree Farm to hang out with her family until it was time for dinner and their planning meeting. Ashley was surprised to see the house in darkness. The front door was locked and she'd forgotten to bring her key. Although the narrow overhanging porch protected her from the rain that'd started, the cold was already seeping into her bones. That left her with two choices of who to land on: Polly and Jack … or Crispin.

As if that was really a question, she thought to herself.

Crispin was startled when someone rapped on the door. He'd been engrossed in an interesting book on Cornish folk singing traditions he'd picked up from the library yesterday. Despite his limited ability to read music, he'd managed to pick out some of the tunes and hoped he might pluck up the nerve to discuss them with Ward sometime. Finding Ashley on the doorstep was an unexpected surprise. 'Oh, hi. You were great on the radio.'

'Thanks.' She peered out from under the hood of her bright red raincoat. 'Do you know where Ward and Nessa are? I assumed they'd be home but there's no one there.'

'They're fine but ... why don't you come in before you freeze?'

'Great idea.' Ashley smiled and stepped in on the mat. 'Oh, that feels wonderful. No Arctic blast blowing through today.'

'It helps that I haven't been cremating any food and I put the gas fire on while I was reading.' In the distraction of seeing her again, he'd almost forgotten why she'd knocked on his door in the first place. 'No one's home at the farmhouse because they almost forgot it was Tristan's two-month check-up this afternoon. Ward texted me after lunch to give me a heads up. They should be back soon. Do you want a coffee?'

'I'd prefer a kiss.'

'Do you want to take your coat off first?'

'Another good idea.' She wriggled out of the wet mac and dropped it to the floor.

One taste of her soft, lush mouth and he was lost again. Crispin recklessly allowed his hands to slide down and cup her backside to press her closer. Her body arched against his and the flush deepened on her pale skin. A sliver of common sense sneaked in and he exhaled a sigh and reluctantly moved away.

'What're you doin'?'

'If you were happy to be whisked away to my bed now, what do you think's going to happen at six o'clock?' She looked puzzled. 'I don't know about you but I'd find it damn near impossible to sit around the kitchen table under the beady eyes of your brother, Nessa, Lowena, Polly and Jack without giving the game away.' He stroked her heated cheek. 'Come back with me tonight.'

'On one condition.' Ashley tilted him a wicked smile. 'I'm not banished to the spare room this time, and yeah I know I did the banishing but that won't happen again.'

'Good.' His rough growl made her laugh.

'Now why don't you fix me a coffee and we'll sit and have a friendly, sensible conversation until dinner time? If nothin' else it'll prove we can.'

Crispin swept into a bow. 'Your wish is my command.'

Ashley made a painstaking effort not to pay special attention to Crispin over dinner and avoided looking his way until Nessa pointed out that the baby whisperer had worked his magic again.

Her poor nephew had been fussy, distinctly unhappy about the jabs he'd received from the doctor and determined to let everyone know it. Nothing soothed him until Crispin offered to hold him, and, within a few minutes, Tristan fell asleep. Crispin made nothing of forking his chicken lasagne in with one hand and jiggling the baby with the other.

'I'll put Tris to bed.' Ward pushed his chair back.

'Do you want me to carry him up?'

Her brother leapt on Crispin's offer, and once the two men disappeared Polly zeroed in on Ashley. A satisfied smirk was plastered all over her face.

'I knew it. I told Jack the other day after you were having dinner with Crispin but he laughed at me.'

Ashley struggled to hide her relief that at least she hadn't been seen leaving Crispin's caravan in the morning.

Polly pointed at Nessa. 'I was right about you and Ward and I've nailed it again.' She shook her head at Ashley. 'Next time you don't want to make something so obvious a young child could spot it, take my advice – ignoring someone you're usually friendly with is a big red flag.'

'What've I missed?' Nessa sounded puzzled.

'We've got another trans-Atlantic romance simmering away with your dear sister-in-law here and a certain handsome ex-soldier.'

'Really? Oh my God, that's wonderful. He's such a great man. I love Crispin.'

Before Ashley could defend herself, or lie, Lowena told them to shush.

'They're coming back.'

'What're you lot up to now?' Ward scrutinised them from the doorway and glanced back over his shoulder at Crispin. 'Probably trouble for us, pal.' Her brother's gaze focused in on his wife again. 'Have we missed something?'

'Yes, but I'd missed it too so don't worry. I'll tell you later. Sit down so we can get on.'

Ashley's embarrassment deepened when Crispin settled in the chair next to her.

Lowena cleared her throat. 'It's the middle of November already which means there's only a little over a fortnight before the first of our festival weekends, but our good news is that all of the food and drink vendors are lined up. We knew most of the larger producers would already be lined up for bigger venues so we've focused on offering low rates to some of the newer ones. It's a win all around because they're grateful to get a foot in the door and it means we have a wide range of unique products on offer. We've got everything from craft gin to clotted cream chocolate. Ashley's taken the lead on all of that so she'll coordinate with Crispin on where the various stalls need to be and he'll take care of the set up and tear down. Kit is coming back to stay at Tregereth with me over his Christmas break from college so we can put him to work for the last two weekends as well.'

Ashley knew her friend couldn't wait to have her son around to spoil. He was only living a few miles away doing a degree in Horticulture and Landscape Design at the Eden Project but didn't have much free time for visiting during the term.

A tiny smile played around the corners of Lowena's mouth. 'She's also worked her magic on the marketing side. I'm sure you all heard her on the radio today doing us proud.'

It was embarrassing when everyone rushed to agree, but she managed to murmur some sort of thanks.

'We've put up posters locally and it's been in all the papers. Polly and Jack have lined up a decent number of amazing craftspeople – again all smaller producers – so they'll also coordinate with Crispin to split them between our two locations. I'll see to the accommodations at Tregereth and the meals we'll serve there, as well as being the overall coordinator. Does anyone have any questions?'

Crispin squeezed her thigh under the table, but she didn't dare to look at him or they'd surely burst out laughing.

Lowena slammed her folder shut. 'Polly's offered to help me clear up dinner so Ward, why don't you take Nessa off and the two of you can relax for a change?'

'We can't take advantage—'

'Yeah, we can.' Her brother's wicked laughter made Nessa turn bright red.

'If I'm no use here, I'll clear off.' Jack smiled at Crispin. 'You ready? We can talk some more about the arrangements while we walk up.'

'Uh, sure.'

'You're staying here.' Polly glared at her clueless husband. 'We need you.'

'What for … oh.' A grin spread over his face when she aimed unsubtle nods at Ashley and Crispin. 'We'll catch up tomorrow, mate.'

'Yeah. Fine.' Crispin pushed his chair back and stood up. She noticed the tips of his ears were pink with embarrassment.

'I'll get out of your way as well.' Ashley gathered up her belongings. 'See y'all later.'

When she stepped outside the door, he was waiting with a wry smile on his face, holding out her mac for her to wriggle back into.

'I hope you haven't changed your mind after that little matchmaking ambush? Military intelligence should put Polly in charge.'

'I'm not that easily put off.'

'Good.' Crispin tugged up her hood. 'Are you ready to be whisked off to my stately home?

'Whisk away.'

Chapter Ten

'Do you want coffee or anything?' Crispin struggled not to pounce on her the minute they stepped inside his caravan.

'Not unless you do. I'm looking at the only thing I want.' The rims of gold in her hazel eyes shone.

'Sorry, I don't mean to be—'

'Thoughtful. Kind. Considerate.' A flare of heat flooded her face. 'If you weren't those things, I wouldn't be so keen.'

'I'm not much of a talker. Never have been. But I want to be different with you.' Emotion thickened his voice.

'Look, I don't want to ruin things by mentioning Bunny – he worked in advertising and could talk until the cows came home, but they were empty words.' She shook her head. 'He convinced me that the way he supposedly loved me was normal. It's goin' to take a while for me to be a hundred per cent sure that was a load of bull.'

He struggled to rein in his anger at the man who'd shaken this amazing woman's confidence so badly that she was still recovering. 'I can't quite believe you're putting your trust in me. Not too many people have done that recently … except for the good ones here. They saved me.'

'You deserved saving. They saw that.' Ashley undid the top button of his navy and red check flannel shirt. 'If it's okay with you, I reckon we've done enough talkin' for now?'

'It's more than okay.' Crispin sensed she needed to take the lead and steeled himself to hold still as she worked her way down the buttons. It wasn't too much of a challenge until she spread open the two sides and smoothed her hand over the thick, dark hair matting his chest.

'I want to touch you everywhere.' Her hushed breath warmed his tightening skin, and he wasn't sure how much more he could stand.

'I won't argue with that.' He somehow dragged out the words. 'Is there any chance you'll invite me into my own bedroom now?'

'I might.'

'Only might?' Crispin stroked her through the soft lilac jumper clinging to her lithe body. Tiny pleading gasps escaped the back of her throat when he slipped his hand underneath the fluffy wool and inched his fingers along her warm skin. 'Bedroom?'

'Yeah.'

They almost tripped over each other stumbling down the narrow corridor and fell on the bed. The sound of their ragged breathing filled the room as they dragged each other's clothes off. He imprinted the picture of her on his mind to dream about later.

'I'm not ... very well endowed.'

Crispin eased her hands away when she tried to cover her breasts. 'You're perfect. I'm no cover model—'

'You're perfect for me and it's all that matters.' She slid him a coy look. 'I'm ready if you are.'

'Hang on a sec.' He almost jerked out the drawer in his bedside table before he found the new package of condoms, but his shaking fingers refused to obey him after that.

'Let me.' Ashley's eyes sparkled as she snatched it away, ripped the box open and offered one packet back to him.

He'd planned to take his time and show her that he might not be the most eloquent man, but he could be tender and thoughtful in bed. That crazy idea disappeared in the ether and Crispin buried himself inside her with the hope that he could at least hold on long enough to satisfy her. He managed with seconds to spare before they collapsed in a satisfied, sweaty heap. 'So, you have a wicked side.' Crispin grinned. 'Who knew?'

The bright morning light streaming in through the half-open blinds woke her. For a few seconds the pale green walls and generic painting of a Cornish tin mine made no sense, until Ashley realised this wasn't *her* bedroom. There was a warm naked man plastered against her back who showed no sign of waking up, but before she had chance to slip out of bed, a firm hand clasped down on her hip.

'And where do you think you're going?'

She wriggled around to meet Crispin's satisfied smile. 'I need to use the bathroom. Is that all right?'

'As long as you come straight back. I've got plans for you.'

'Mmm, I can only imagine.' Ashley glanced down at her phone and groaned. 'Oh God, have you any idea what time it is?'

'Not really. Can't say I care either.'

She thrust the screen in his face. 'It's nine o'clock. Lowena will kill me.'

'*Nine*? I never sleep that late.'

'Yeah, well, you didn't exactly *sleep* all those hours, did you?' The playful observation made him chuckle. 'I'll pop in the bathroom a minute, but then I have to go.'

'You'll be back?'

'Tonight, if you'll have me?'

His sexy grin returned. 'Oh, I can promise that.' Crispin threw back the covers then glowered at her. 'Stop that.'

She'd been checking out his rugged body. 'Why?'

'Because you won't bloody well make it out of here anytime soon if you don't.'

'Is that a threat or a promise?' Ashley laughed and grabbed her clothes before he could stop her, then dived into the miniature bathroom. It was pointless to shower because she didn't have any clean clothes so all she could do was wash her face and smear some of his toothpaste over her teeth. 'That's me done ...' She was surprised to find the bedroom empty and wandered out to the kitchen, fully expecting to discover him making tea but he wasn't there either. Two deep men's voices drifted in through the thin walls, and although one was definitely Crispin, she didn't recognise the other. Ashley shoved her feet in her shoes, found her handbag and coat and opened the caravan door. Her new lover stood head-to-head with a stranger whose cropped dark hair and air of control immediately made her think "military".

'Oh hi, I wondered where you were.' They both appeared startled and she got the distinct impression of having interrupted something important. Crispin rearranged his stern features into a smile and hurriedly shoved an envelope in his pocket.

'Come and meet Aled Jones. He's an old mate from the army. A fellow Welshman.'

They swapped a few minutes of ordinary pleasant conversation – the "where do you come from and what do you think of England?" variety. Aled made her laugh when he explained about Crispin's regimental nickname: Cornflake.

'I'd love to chat some more, but I'd better be off to work.

I'll see you later.' A faint flush of colour warmed Crispin's cheeks. 'It was good to meet you, Aled.' She strode off down the gravel path but couldn't help wondering if she'd been wrong to expect a kiss or some sort of acknowledgement from Crispin. She was too preoccupied on the walk back to Tregereth to admire the view, but her pace slowed as she approached the house. Its old stone walls were bathed in muted winter sunshine, and the fresh white paint picked out the elegance of the tall Georgian windows. Cornwall's temperate climate meant there were always signs of life in the gardens, and even now the shiny, dark green leaves of the camellias and magnolias were interspersed with pops of colour from the last of the bronze chrysanthemums. If the weather cooperated, she knew they'd see daffodils blooming at Christmas.

Lowena flung open the front door, holding a sweeping brush in one hand. 'There you are! I was about to send out a search party.'

'Sorry, I—'

'Don't apologise. I'm glad you had a good time.' Her friend's scrutiny deepened. 'It *was* good, wasn't it?'

'Yeah. Great.'

'Well, if that's how you sound when you've enjoyed yourself, I'd hate to hear you when you're miserable.'

'I'm tired, that's all.' Her smile felt tight and fake. 'I desperately need a shower.'

'I'll get us a coffee sorted for when you come down.'

'Thanks.' Ashley disappeared to the sanctuary of her bedroom. By the time a hot shower pounded some sense into her, she'd come to the rueful conclusion that she'd overreacted. It had been juvenile to expect Crispin to be all over her in front of an old friend, and the men's awkwardness was probably nothing more than army talk they didn't feel comfortable about sharing. The mouth-watering aroma of bacon frying made her stomach rumble and sent her rushing back down to the kitchen.

'I thought you could do with a proper breakfast instead of your usual twigs and seeds.' Her friend set down a plate loaded with a traditional English cooked breakfast: something she knew Ashley rarely ate.

She didn't argue but gave the fried egg a satisfying poke to make the yolk run over the plate before she started to dig in.

'Something, or should I say someone, has taken *your* restrained appetite away and replaced it with a navvy's. More coffee?'

'Please.'

'I've planned out the Christmas decorations for the guest bedrooms, so I thought we'd make a start today with spray painting pine cones gold for the mantles, then do simple artificial wreaths for each door. We can add candles and fresh greenery inside the rooms closer to the time.' She folded her arms. 'Before we get to work, are you going to tell me what's up? Did Crispin do anything out of line? I know we're all fond of him but he's got his demons and—'

'No, absolutely not. He was wonderful.' She needed her thoughts either confirmed or laughed at. 'Have you ever heard him mention a man called Aled Jones?'

'Aled?' Lowena frowned. 'Yes, but I haven't met him. I think he's the person who convinced Crispin to turn himself back into the army and spoke up for him so they let him off lightly. Why do you ask?'

She poured out the whole story. 'Am I making something of nothing?'

'Maybe. You need to ask Crispin to be frank with you tonight. If you're not satisfied with his answer, you'll have to decide your next move.'

'Thanks.' She surprised her friend with a hug. 'Lead me to the pine cones.' Lowena's summing up made complete sense, but the suspicion that she might not like Crispin's answer wouldn't go away. The secretive looks she'd seen him exchange with Aled Jones stayed in her mind, nagging like a sore tooth.

Chapter Eleven

Ashley spotted Crispin sitting on the caravan steps and staring into space as she approached,

'You should join the SAS. I didn't hear you coming.' His head jerked up. 'How's your day been anyway?'

'Busy.' She waved her hands in his face, pointing out the multitude of tiny cuts and traces of gold paint all over them. 'Lowena started me off easy with artificial wreaths for the bedroom doors, then we collected and sprayed pine cones before she upped the ante. She wants holly wreaths in every one of the front windows at Tregereth and here at Nessa's before the festival weekends start so we had a practise run.' Ashley waggled her sore fingers. 'She also taught me the art of bow making and if I never see another reel of red satin ribbon, it'll suit me fine.' All set to carry on chattering, she suddenly realised he looked glum. 'What's up with you? You look as though you've lost a hundred-dollar bill and found a dime.'

He heaved a sigh. 'I've been pissing people off. Ward and Polly both got the sharp edge of my tongue. After that I dug the garden to stay out of everyone's way.'

'Because?'

'Aled brought me some ... unsettling ... news this morning.'

'Are you gonna share it with me?'

Crispin dragged himself up to standing and pushed the caravan door open. 'Let's go in. I'll stick the kettle on.'

'Oh yeah, that'll help a bunch.' A wry smile curved the edges of his mouth. 'Y'all can't do without those pesky hot drinks. I mean I love my coffee as much as the next person, but I don't need regular infusions every few hours.' She brushed past him and shucked her dark green wool coat off, putting it on the arm of the sofa before sitting down. Today's colder weather reminded her they were well into November and that back home her parents would be celebrating Thanksgiving next week. Only after that did the countdown to Christmas really start.

He bypassed the kitchen and joined her. 'I told you once I'd been involved with a woman several years ago and we both got hurt.' Crispin absently rubbed a hand over his bristly chin. 'Her name was Samira. I hadn't heard from her again ... until Aled brought me some news about her today.'

'Bad news?'

'Not exactly.' His craggy face sunk into deep furrows. 'Samira was an intelligence officer in my battalion on my last deployment to Afghanistan. She worked mostly as an interpreter because her maternal grandmother was born in Kabul and she'd been brought up bilingual. We became good friends ... and then more.'

'Was she married?'

He turned paler. 'No, but our relationship was against army regulations.' Crispin shrugged his powerful shoulders. 'Her father is a brigadier and he was furious when word got back to him. He wasn't about to have Samira's career affected, so I was thrown on the first flight back to the UK.'

'That was harsh. What happened to Samira?'

'Aled works in the Adjutant's office and this arrived a few days ago.' He dragged a crumpled envelope from his pocket. 'Well, the original did. This is a copy. He could get in big trouble for circumventing official channels.'

'He's your friend. Cornflake.' Ashley's feeble attempt at a joke fell flat. Her heart raced when he held out the envelope. 'Sure?'

'Yep.' He shoved it in her hand.

She scanned the brief letter and the bottom dropped out of her world. 'Oh Crispin. What're you goin' to do?'

That was the million-dollar question.

'You'll bring them here.' Ashley's frankness pulled a faint smile out of him.

Samira's letter asked the regiment for Crispin's forwarding address so she could let him know she was now living in Oxfordshire with her son – an almost four-year-old little boy named Rhys.

'Rhys is my middle name.' His voice cracked.

'Why didn't she ask her father to help find you?'

'Apparently they had a massive argument after he had me sent away. I'm guessing he doesn't know that I'm supposedly Rhys's father.'

'Supposedly? Ashley's scathing look told him that was a monumental blunder. 'Why would you doubt her?'

Crispin shrugged. Apologies. Explanations. Pleas for compassion. All of those stuck in his throat.

'Let me know when you've decided to do the right thing by them both.' She unravelled her legs and stood up.

Without another word she walked out and he did nothing to stop her.

There were only two things he could imagine doing right now. After he left Afghanistan, he'd made a conscious choice not to drink for his own well-being, but if he stayed here it might be impossible to resist. That left option two.

He retreated to the bedroom and dragged his backpack out of the wardrobe. It didn't take long to gather up the belongings he needed before he changed into his old hiking clothes and sat on the edge of the bed to lace up his worn leather boots. Crispin yanked on his heavy camouflage jacket and hoisted the bag on his shoulders. He scribbled a quick note to put in Ward and Nessa's letterbox and was swept by a brief pang of regret when he locked the caravan on his way out. Whether he'd be welcome on his return when Ashley told everyone the reason why he left was debatable.

The sound of his heavy footsteps crunching across the gravel outside the farm house ricocheted like gunshots and he held his breath when the metal flap banged after he slid the note through the letterbox. No one came out so he sprinted towards the gate and on up the hill. He kept up the same fast pace until he'd passed Tregereth House so he couldn't be tempted to make a detour. In his army days he routinely ran for miles carrying a similar load, but he'd become soft and the straps were already chafing his shoulders. Crispin settled into a brisk walk until he crested the hill at the top of Penmeor Road, where he came to a stop and peered out over a low spot in the hedge. The moonlight hanging over the distant coast picked up orange and gold tips on the pitch-black waves, reminding him of his old friend Polly's hair. A sliver of sadness lodged in his gut. Was he doomed to keep disappointing people?

He trudged on.

Chapter Twelve

'So, what's the story?' Ward burst into the kitchen at Tregereth waving a piece of paper around.

'Is somethin' wrong?' Ashley sipped her breakfast coffee.

'According to this, Crispin left last night and he says to ask you why. Did the two of you have a bust up of some sort?' He pushed a letter across the table.

The writing was as firm, dark and decisive as the man himself, the slashes of black ink almost ground into the paper. All it said was that he was fine but would be gone for a few days and to ask her if they wanted any further information. A flash of annoyance pulled at Ashley.

'For a start, I didn't know he'd gone – but it's nothing to do with me.' That wasn't totally true but it was all she planned on telling her brother.

'We don't need this right now.' Ward slumped on the nearest chair. 'Nessa's out of her mind with worry.'

'I'm sure she is and I'm sorry. When he comes back, he can explain as much as he wants then.'

'If I assume a worst-case scenario and he's not back by next week, who's going to take over his jobs? He was goin' to knock up the booths for the Christmas craft and food vendors. I'm crap at carpentry, and if we've gotta pay someone it'll eat into our profits.'

'That won't be necessary.' Lowena stopped scrubbing the sink. 'I'm handy with a saw and Jack can turn his hand to anything. We'll manage between us.'

'You?'

Her brother's dismissive question made Ashley wince.

'Yes, me.' She swung around, hands on hips and glared at Ward. 'My ex-husband was useless when it came to DIY, so I learned to do anything that needed doing.'

'I'm sorry. I didn't mean to imply—'

'You most certainly did.'

Ashley felt a brief flicker of sympathy for her brother before deciding he deserved it and sat back to enjoy herself. After an inordinate amount of grovelling, he was let off the hook.

'I'll come back to the farm with you and talk to Jack.' Lowena peeled off her rubber gloves and untied her apron. 'We'll make a list of the supplies we need, and I assume you can manage to pick them up in Truro?' The implication hovered in the air that something so simple shouldn't be beyond his capabilities.

'Yeah, no problem.' Ward glanced at Ashley. 'You gonna be okay?'

'Why wouldn't I?'

He coloured to the roots of his hair. 'I dunno, just thought you might be—'

'Pissed at Crispin? Yeah, I am, but I'm not gonna sit around moping. I've got signs and leaflets to work on so I'll be glued to the computer most of the day. Off you both go. I'll be fine.'

After the front door closed behind them, Ashley hunched over with her head sunk into her hands. Fear crept in that their fragile new relationship might not survive this.

Crispin didn't doubt that they'd all think he was a coward – particularly Ashley – but walking was the healthiest way he'd discovered to cope with life's problems. Over the last few years, he'd hiked large chunks of the 630-mile South West Coast Path, but he'd never tackled the North Cornwall section. Now seemed as good a time as any to knock out the challenging sixty-six-mile stretch.

His calves were protesting at the unaccustomed stretching he'd put them through since yesterday. After he'd left Pear Tree Farm, he'd walked into Truro and caught the late bus to Newquay, camped in a field outside the town then hit the coastal path as soon as the sun came up this morning. Most of today's twenty-four-mile stretch from Newquay through Porthcothan and onto Padstow was a slog in cold, persistent drizzle which suited his dour mood. The combination of lousy weather and the time of year meant there were very few other fools on the trail.

Now he'd treated himself to a pitch at a small campsite in order to have a hot shower and dry out his wet clothes. If he hadn't been an idiot, he could be in his comfortable caravan now with a warm, naked woman snuggled up with him instead of huddled in his tent and burrowed down in his sleeping bag to stay warm.

Like that would be true, you moron, he thought.

Crispin couldn't remember the last time he'd thought about Samira. Their relationship was intense but short-lived, and he suspected the constant need for secrecy had ramped up the desirability factor on both sides. They'd never even had the opportunity to say goodbye. He did consider writing to her before deciding that might make a bad situation worse. Afterwards, his personal problems deteriorated to the point where going AWOL had seemed to be the only way to survive, and by the time he emerged on the other side of that Samira had faded to a footnote in his life.

Aled's letter changed everything. Now he couldn't get her and little Rhys out of his head.

The glowing red numbers on his watch said five o'clock, and at this time of year it wouldn't be daylight and safe enough to start walking until close to eight. It shouldn't be too bad as far as Port Isaac but the stretch from there to King Arthur's castle was supposed to be gruelling, and Crispin suspected it would take all he had to make it to Tintagel before dark.

It was pointless to lay here feeling sorry for himself, so he'd pack up his tent and stroll into Padstow to find a café. A decent cooked breakfast should set him up for another day of hard walking and even harder thinking.

If she stared at the computer any longer her eyes would explode. Today's thick drizzle wasn't letting up anytime soon, but she was over being a wimp about the Cornish weather. Ashley headed down to the hall and sat down on the wooden bench Crispin had made for their guests to use when changing their shoes. She kicked off her soft black flats and tugged on her newest purchase – bright red rubber boots splashed with cheerful yellow flowers.

'*You need wellies. Got to get with the programme.*'

The man wouldn't leave her alone.

Gusts of cold, rain-soaked wind whipped around her when she stepped out of the house, and by the time she battled her way to the bottom of Penmeor Road, Ashley had aborted her plan to go into the village. It seemed more appealing to beg a hot cup of coffee off Nessa and play with little Tristan.

'What're you doing out in this weather?' Polly accosted her as she walked through the farm gate.

'I fancied some fresh air.'

'There's no shortage of that today.' She nodded towards the farmhouse. 'If you were thinking of stopping in to see them, they've gone Christmas shopping in Truro. I'm just off home to put the kettle on. Come and have a cup with me. It'll give you a chance to dry out before you trek back up the road again.'

'Thanks.' Ashley felt cornered. This was handing her friend a golden opportunity to pump her about Crispin's disappearance.

'I'll make us both a coffee. I know you're not a tea-drinker. Come on.' Polly marched away which left her no choice but to trudge along behind.

They stuck their wet boots and macs in the caravan's bathroom out of the way, and Polly soon had the gas fire burning and their drinks made.

'Sit down and 'ave a bit of saffron cake. You could do with some more meat on your bones.'

Ashley obediently took a slice of pale yellow cake dotted with dried fruit. She'd been fooled before by English cakes because they often looked sweeter than they turned out to be. This time her first bite confirmed that Polly's offering delivered on its visual promise to be hard and uninteresting.

'Where's our boy gone to then?'

She almost choked on the dry cake. 'I honestly don't know.'

'I thought he'd got all that hiking around out of his

system. I mean Jack and me love nothing better than a good walk along the coast, but at this time of year?' Her sympathetic eyes rested on Ashley. 'If you want to talk, it won't go any further than these four walls.' Polly patted her hand. 'I like a bit of gossip as much as the next person, but I also know how to keep a secret.'

Ashley knew this was true, because until last year no one in Cornwall knew about the little boy Polly and Jack had lost decades ago in a tragic fire. She couldn't keep it to herself any longer and poured everything out.

'Was I wrong to say that to him?'

'Do you think so now?'

'Yes and no. I could've phrased it better.' She heaved a sigh. 'In a kinder way.' Ashley swiped at her eyes with the sleeve of her jumper.

'You can put things straight when he comes back.'

'But what if he doesn't?'

She realised that was her worst nightmare.

Chapter Thirteen

Crispin slapped a fresh plaster over his blister and tugged on a pair of clean socks. The last two days had pushed him to his limits, but the army had honed his stubborn nature, turning perseverance into a determination to withstand anything thrown at him.

On Saturday the bad weather never let up, and there were places on the gruelling stretch from Port Isaac to Tintagel where he'd barely been able to make out the crumbling cliff edge through the driving rain, but yesterday he'd seen a glimmer of hope when he'd woken up to watery blue skies and a stiff breeze blowing in off the Atlantic. The morning's first six miles to Boscastle were relatively easy before he slogged through five hours of steep climbs and rough terrain to reach Crackington Haven.

That morning he'd eaten breakfast stretched out on the grass outside his tent and was happily contemplating the view spread out in front of him that resembled a watercolour painting. The tiny village was dappled with early morning sunshine and the sandy cove was deserted apart from a couple of dog walkers. He was almost tempted to go down for a walk on the beach, but it would hinder the plans he'd made last night to pound out the last twenty miles. He'd already decided that afterwards he would head back to Polgarth and whatever might face him there.

'You fancy a cuppa?' A tall, sandy-haired man strolled over from an old rusty caravan and held out an enamel mug.

'Cheers.' Crispin checked out his fellow camper's lean, worn face, wispy beard and unkempt clothes. 'You been stopped here long or just walking the path like me?' The stranger's blue eyes turned wary. 'Crispin Davies, ex-army, Royal Welsh Regiment.' He cracked a smile. 'Better known as Cornflake.'

'Ralph White – goes without saying they call me Chalky – Royal Marines. Ex too … kind of.' His gaze was troubled. 'I'd better be off. Leave the mug outside when you're done.'

In his head, Crispin heard Ashley ordering him to have some guts. 'I don't know your story and it's none of my business unless you're interested in sharing it, but I went on the run about three years ago. Bummed around a bit. Found refuge at a campsite between Truro and Redruth. Long story short, an old mate talked me into going back and clearing things with the army.'

'Good for you.'

He ignored the flash of sarcasm. 'I'm not looking over my shoulder all the time now. Makes a hell of a difference.' Crispin unzipped one of his backpack pockets and fished out the small notebook he carried to keep track of his hikes. He scrawled down his name and the address of Pear Tree Farm. 'If you need any help, get in touch. I'll do what I can.'

The man wordlessly snatched the paper and stalked off.

A tiny smile pulled at his mouth. Perhaps Nessa could turn her campsite into a no-questions-asked shelter for disillusioned servicemen? Crispin yanked his boots on and laced them up. *Time to get going.* He had bridges to repair.

'Is there any chance I might get an answer sometime today?' Lowena's sharp voice penetrated Ashley's mental fog. 'What do you think of the stalls we've made?'

They were standing in the old barn behind Nessa's house.

'Awesome. Very fancy. I didn't expect them to have roofs.' Trust Lowena to take the idea of simple wooden stalls for the craft and food vendors and turn it up multiple notches.

'They'll protect people from the worst of the weather. Outside events in Cornwall are always risky.' A tight smile lifted her expression. 'The roofs are detachable.'

They would be, thought Ashley. *No one else would go to all that trouble.*

'If we were only using them for the Christmas fair, I would've painted them in festive colours but I chose the neutral dark stain so they'll be handy for other events. We'll decorate them with lights and greenery.'

At a guess she'd be the one whipping those up.

'I assume you haven't heard from Crispin?'

'Uh no. I would've told you.'

'Would you? You've barely spoken since last Thursday when we found out he'd gone, unless it's about the festival. Don't bother to spin that ridiculous story again about not knowing why he left either because we both know that's a lie. I thought we were close.' The hurt in her voice was unmistakeable.

Ashley wrangled with her conscience but couldn't bring herself to speak.

'Fair enough. Keep it to yourself. I'm off to do more baking for the freezer. Are you coming?'

'I'll be up soon after I pop in to see Nessa and Tris for a few minutes. You've done an awesome job with the stalls.' The sop to Lowena's ego earned her a fleeting nod.

It always felt awkward to walk straight into the farmhouse, but they'd told her to do that instead of knocking on the door or ringing the bell and risk waking a sleeping baby. She always made sure to rattle the latch and stomp her feet on the mat so there was less chance of catching her brother and his wife unawares.

'We're in the kitchen,' Nessa shouted. 'A certain little boy needs a cuddle with Aunty Ash. He's bored of his mummy.'

'Is he? Hand him over.' She swooped down to pick up her grizzling nephew. He'd recently started to smile and treated her to a glorious one that melted her heart.

'Biological clock ticking? Oh sorry … that was tactless.'

Very few people knew about the early miscarriage she'd suffered shortly before her marriage broke up, but her sister-in-law was one of those people.

'It's okay. Honestly.' She'd experienced a few wistful moments since Tristan's arrival, but the vulnerability and wonder of a new-born baby tugged at most people unless they had hearts of stone.

'I don't suppose you've heard from—'

'Crispin? No.'

'Sorry.'

A sigh slipped out. 'No, *I'm* sorry.' She stroked Tris's downy head and he snuggled in the crook of her shoulder.

'He did something to upset you, didn't he?'

Ashley ignored the question and carried on babbling nonsense to the baby and playing with his plump little fingers.

'No one's perfect and we all make mistakes.'

She kept her voice even. 'It's something we have to sort out ourselves.'

'You know I'm only asking because we care about you both.'

'I know.' Reluctantly, she handed her nephew back over. 'I should go. Lowena's to-do list is calling.'

'Are we okay?'

'Of course.' Not a hundred per cent true, but her kind-hearted sister-in-law would stay awake tonight fretting if she thought she'd upset Ashley. 'What's that for?' A pile of colourful plaid material was piled on one end of the kitchen table.

'In a moment of madness, I bought it to make scarves for us all to wear for the Christmas festival weekends. I'm afraid my ambitious plans didn't take this little monster into account.' Nessa kissed the top of Tristan's head.

'It's cute. Not very Christmassy though.'

'That's because it's the Cornish national tartan. The white cross on a black background is from the banner of Saint Piran, the patron saint of tinners. Black and gold are the colours of the ancient Cornish kings, red is for the legs and beak of the national bird, the Cornish chough, and blue for the blue of the sea surrounding Cornwall.' Nessa broke into a wide grin. 'That's your local history lesson for the day.'

'Awesome.' Ashley fingered the material. 'I could make them if you like?'

'I didn't know you sewed?'

'Yeah, I used to love it … but I haven't done any for a while.' Bunny had mocked her for making her own clothes when they first met so she put her sewing machine away. The first thing she did when she decided to stay longer in Cornwall was go out and buy a new one.

'If you've got the time, that would be amazing.'

'I'll make time.' There wouldn't be any long wonderful nights with Crispin in the foreseeable future, so she might as well put the empty hours to good use.

'There are some plastic carrier bags hanging up behind that door.' Nessa pointed towards the larder. 'Help yourself.'

Ashley stuffed the material into a couple of bags and left the house with a new spring in her step.

Crispin stared at his phone and debated for about the twentieth time whether or not to make the call. The weather had been tolerable, but he hadn't paced himself for the last twenty miles of his self-imposed challenge so now every bone in his body screamed at him.

He rubbed at his cramped right hamstring. Somehow, he'd made it to Marsland Mouth – the end or beginning of the North Cornwall stretch of the South West Coastal Path depending which way someone tackled the trail. The pebbly beach that lay somewhere out in front of him in the dark marked the county boundary between Devon to the north and Cornwall to the south.

Decision time. He tapped in Ward's number and sagged with relief to hear his friend's American accent loud and clear. 'I need a lift home if you can manage it?'

'Sure thing. Are you okay?'

'Yep. I am now.'

The two of them rarely discussed anything outside of work, but running through their friendship was the knowledge that, in different ways, they both owed their lives to Nessa and Pear Tree Farm.

'Where are you?'

Crispin filled him in on the details. There was no vehicle access at Marsland Mouth so the safest thing was for him to walk back to the car park at Welcombe Mouth. The luminous dial on his watch reminded him how late it was. 'Look, mate, I've had second thoughts. It'll take you the best part of an hour and a half to drive here and I don't want Nessa fretting because you're out on unfamiliar roads. I'll stick my tent up for the night, and you can come in the morning instead.'

'If it was the other way around and I was doin' the asking, would you come?'

'Well, yeah but—'

'But nothing.'

Crispin smiled. 'Cheers.'

'I'll call when I'm gettin' close.' Ward rang off.

Crispin hefted his backpack on and trudged off down the road. In a few hours he'd be home again.

Chapter Fourteen

'You're a hard woman to track down.'

Ashley almost ran the sewing machine needle through her finger and jerked around. 'Oh … it's you.' Crispin hovered in the doorway throwing her an anxious look. She couldn't decide whether to run over and throw her arms around him for being safe and in one piece, or smack him from here to John O'Groats for the worry he'd caused them all. 'When did you get back?'

'Late last night. Ward gave me a lift.'

Seriously? Her brother hadn't said a word.

'Don't blame him.'

'Why not?'

'I asked him not to tell anyone.' Crispin shuffled from one foot to the other. 'I don't mean you especially.'

'Where've you been?'

'I walked the North Cornwall stretch of the coastal path. Sixty-six miles since Friday morning. It about killed me. Maybe you wish it had?'

Part of her would give anything to say yes. Truthfully, all she wanted was to brush away the straggle of dark hair from his face and soothe the waves of exhaustion pulsing off him.

'Sunday morning in Crackington Haven I met a poor guy who reminded me so much of myself a few years ago, it was uncanny. I'd stopped at this small campsite for the night and had just finished eating my breakfast when a young chap wandered over to speak. I introduced myself and said I was ex-army and he told me his name was

Chalky White, and it seemed that he was on the run from the Royal Marines.' His voice thickened. 'I wasn't sure how much to say but I thought about you and guessed you'd tell me to step up.'

Ashley gamely tried to suppress a smile.

'I briefly ran through my own story and wrote down my name and the address of the farm. I encouraged him to come here if he ever wants help … although I'm not sure how Nessa will react if he does turn up.' He looked worried.

'You know she'd make him welcome. We all would.'

'Yeah, I know that really … but I keep going over it in my head and wondering if I could've done anything more.'

'Don't beat yourself up.' Ashley hated to see him so down on himself. 'You know better than anyone that he's got to get there in his own time.'

'I missed you more than you'll ever know. You were right about Samira and the boy. The news took me from the ground up, that's all, and I needed to get things straight in my head. I won't turn my back on them, I promise.' His voice turned raspy. 'Oh for God's sake, don't cry. Please.' He strode across the room and hauled her up into his arms. 'I'd rather walk every one of those damn sixty-six miles again than see you in tears.'

The clean scent of shampoo drifted down from his hair, and she couldn't resist running her fingers through the chunky thickness at the nape of his neck. 'I was so damn worried about you. Don't you dare do that again.'

Crispin tilted her a sad smile. 'Nessa said the same thing the last time I went off. Is she mad too?'

'Everyone was concerned – and I didn't appreciate you dropping me in it with them all.'

'Sorry.' His thick eyebrows beetled together. 'How did they take the news?'

'I didn't tell them. It wasn't my place.' That stretched the truth somewhat, but she'd sworn Polly to secrecy.

'Oh right. Now it makes sense why Ward seemed puzzled last night when I rambled on about taking time off to go to Oxfordshire. He promised it wouldn't be a problem but he didn't ask any questions. Awesome bloke, your brother.'

'Not a problem?' Ashley's voice rose. 'He was being his usual generous self. You need to ask Lowena and Jack how many hours they've put in to build the stalls you were supposed to make. Ward's neglected other jobs to cover your normal everyday work too.' It was important he understood how crucial his contribution was to the businesses. 'The work you do matters.'

'And what about all this?' Crispin pointed to her sewing.

'I can't blame you for that because I volunteered.' Her brief explanation made him smile until she mentioned having more time because he wasn't around. Ashley watched the wheels spin in his head. This was a turning point for them, and he knew it.

Asking for help didn't come naturally but he refused to screw up the best thing that had happened to him in forever. 'I'm really sorry for everything. Will you help me fix it? I need to find a way to tell them all about Aled's visit and the letter, but I'm not sure how to go about it.'

'I'll do everything I can. Polly assured me I could put things right when you returned so that's what I ...' Ashley turned pale.

'You told Polly about me? That's not what you said

just now.' Crispin couldn't hide his horror. He listened to her stammered out explanation, and it wasn't difficult to picture her cornered by their old friend and coerced into spilling the beans.

'I'm so sorry, but it about killed me not having anyone to talk to and she was there and ...' She flung out her hands in a gesture of helplessness.

'Forget it. It's all my fault. I've been an idiot.'

'Well yeah, pretty much.' She nestled back into him. 'You need to treat it like a loose tooth when you were little.'

'Huh?'

'Were you a wriggler or yank it out sort of boy?'

He smiled. 'You're saying I should get it over with and tell everyone in one go?'

'Yep. So everyone's tired, right?' The gold flecks in Ashley's eyes sparkled. 'Mrs Sampson at the shop has started selling pizzas in the evenings. They're pretty damn good and it pisses off Benjy at the pub so it's a win all around. You could offer to treat everyone to dinner. Perhaps suggest we gather at the farmhouse so Nessa and Ward don't have to worry about Tris?'

Crispin was dubious. 'So, while we stuff ourselves with pepperoni pizza, I drop into the conversation that I had an affair with one of my superior officers while I was in Afghanistan and I've got an almost four-year-old son I didn't know anything about?' He grimaced. 'Oh, and she's tracked me down and wants to meet?'

'I could invite them all if you like? Might be less awkward.' She threw him a searching look. 'Did I hear a big thank you?'

'You snatched the words from my mouth.' Crispin

brushed a soft kiss over her lips and nuzzled her neck. 'Do those scarves *have* to be finished today?'

'Absolutely.' She wriggled away but looked more satisfied than cross. 'We've only got a few days before the festival starts, and I need to make some phone calls before people make dinner plans. I'll let you know what they say and if we're on for tonight, you're in charge of ordering the food and picking it up.'

'Yes, ma'am.' His fake drawl made her roll her eyes. 'I'll leave you alone and get busy with some work.'

'About time.' Ashley shooed him off with a bright smile. He took that as a win.

It wasn't often she felt homesick these days, but when she hung up the phone a short while later after talking with her parents, Ashley's throat was tight with unshed tears. Fiona had chattered non-stop about all the cooking she'd done ready for Thanksgiving in a couple of days. That made Ashley nostalgic for the family celebrations of her childhood, and now she could almost taste Aunt Lila's bourbon pecan pie, her cousin May's cornbread dressing and the golden-brown turkey fried by her father out on the patio no matter what the weather.

The fact she'd see her folks in about another three weeks when they arrived in Cornwall for Christmas didn't lift her mood.

'Are you ready?' Lowena's voice drifted up the stairs. 'I don't want to be late.'

Anyone would think they were going to a state dinner at Buckingham Palace instead of a casual pizza supper in Nessa's kitchen. Ashley had made an effort though by changing into pale grey trousers that she paired with a deep rose-pink cashmere jumper before taking a few extra seconds to slick on a layer of pink lipstick. If she was lucky, it would get kissed off later. Ashley smiled and headed on down. 'All present and correct, ma'am.'

'Cheeky girl.'

They stowed the Christmas festival signs they'd made on the back seat of Lowena's car and fitted several boxes of catering supplies in the boot.

'I'm assuming Crispin is behind this dinner invitation, so does that mean we find out the mystery behind his disappearance? Those of us who don't know already that is.'

Ashley shrugged and ignored the pointed questions. Everyone's curiosity would be satisfied soon and she wasn't cracking now.

As soon as they parked, her brother came out to help unload, and over his shoulder she spotted Polly and Jack walking down to join them.

'Crispin shouldn't be long; he's left to fetch the pizzas.' Polly said. 'Isn't this kind of him?'

'It sure is.' Ashley avoided looking directly at her friend. They were the only people who knew the truth behind tonight's get-together. She escaped into the chaos of Nessa's warm, comfortable kitchen and made herself useful by laying the table, making it easier to stay out of the various conversations going on.

'Pizza delivery.' Crispin arrived carrying several steaming cardboard boxes that he set down in the middle of the well-scrubbed oak table.

Following the unwritten rules, they'd all settled in their

familiar spots. Polly faced the window with Jack and Lowena taking up the rest of the space on that side of the table. Nessa sat closest to the range cuddling a sleepy baby with Ward next to her. Crispin pulled out the chair by Ashley and immediately reached for her hand, giving it a warm squeeze. While they ate, all of the conversation revolved around the Christmas festival plans.

'I'm going to put Tris to bed.' Nessa stood up. 'Don't you dare talk about anything important until I get back.' She flung Crispin a warning glare.

Polly filled the time by retelling all of the gossip she'd picked in Polgarth over the last few days, including the fact her friend Dorrie had knitted a bunch of tea-cosies for the church stall at the festival. 'Ugly things they are – all bobbles and dropped stitches. I've got several hidden away in a drawer at home already. She makes them for every sale we have.'

'Are we talking about the dreaded tea-cosies? Poor Dorrie means well but they are awful!' Nessa flopped back down in her chair and held her wine glass out for Ward to refill. 'Thanks so much for dinner, Crispin. You didn't have to do this.'

'I wanted to. It's my way of apologising for going off that way and neglecting my work. I appreciate all of you for filling in for me.' His voice thickened. 'The main reason *why* I needed to go is harder to explain.' His grip on her hand tightened. 'You all either know or know of Aled Jones. Last week he brought me a letter which … unsettled me.' The whole story poured out and, although the first part about his relationship with Samira didn't raise too many eyebrows, when he told them about Rhys a shocked gasp ran around the room. 'I didn't take the news well, but this sweet lady—' he nodded at Ashley '—she put me straight, or at least she tried to. I got a warning to step up or—'

'She wouldn't share your bed again.' Ward chuckled. 'Good on ya, Ash.'

Her face flamed.

'I should think so too.' Lowena's uncompromising tone made everyone smile. 'So, what's your plan?'

'I'm not quite sure.' Crispin's brow furrowed. 'When I got back yesterday, I was all set to hare off to Oxfordshire to see them, but I think I need to get in touch with Samira first and go from there?' His gaze rested on her. 'Does that sound reasonable?'

Knowing he valued her opinion brought a lump to her throat. 'Absolutely. Maybe send her a letter first? It could be easier than an awkward phone conversation.'

'You know we'll support you however it works out.' Nessa smiled at him. 'Another little boy in our special community here would be awesome.'

Crispin's eyes were glassy with tears. 'Sorry.'

'Nothing to be sorry for, mate.' Jack reached across and patted his arm. 'You aren't the only one who found a home and family here in hard times.' He smiled at Nessa. 'She's the best.'

'Yeah, she sure is.' Ward's look was one of pure adoration.

This was what I wanted, Ashley thought. After she'd extricated herself from her marriage, she'd sworn never to trust anyone ever again but since meeting the wonderful man sitting beside her again, she was allowing herself to hope.

'If there's anything we can do to help, you must tell us.' Polly sounded fierce. 'No more keeping things to yourself, you silly boy.'

Crispin grinned. 'I promise.'

'I've got a darts match at the pub.' Jack announced. 'Polly's coming, and if anyone else fancies a drink I'd appreciate the moral support.'

'Lowena, why don't you and Nessa go along?' Ward suggested. 'There's a programme on Cornish mining at eight o'clock I want to watch. I'll listen out for Tris.'

Ashley leaned over to whisper in Crispin's ear. 'I can think of better ways to occupy our evening.'

'All right, you pair.' Jack chuckled. 'I'd say get a room but a caravan works too.'

Ribald comments flew around the table like ping pong balls.

'Come on, let's leave these children to it.' Ashley stood up and held out her hand to Crispin whose face was wreathed in a sheepish smile.

'Better do as I'm told.'

'That's a good start.' Ward winked at them. 'You're gettin' him well trained.'

Ashley almost dragged him from the kitchen. 'You'd better make all of that embarrassment worthwhile.' She didn't honestly think that would be an issue.

Chapter Fifteen

Crispin snatched the letter out of Nessa's hand. 'I've been waiting for this. I know it's only been a little over a week but—'

'You were getting anxious.'

'I'd better wait and read it later. Ward and I are off soon to borrow Jago Teague's trailer to go to the Christmas tree farm. It's got to be done this morning so we've got time to install them in their assigned spots ready to be decorated tomorrow. Lowena's orders.'

'Don't be daft. My sister won't know if you delay a few minutes.' She hitched her wriggling son back up on her hip.

'I wouldn't bet on it.'

'We'll leave you alone.'

'Tell Ward I'll be down soon.' They both knew he needed to find out Samira's reply right now. Crispin had tried to give her a measured response, but who knew how she'd taken it? His heart raced as he slit open the envelope with a pocketknife. Tears pricked his eyes as he pulled out a small, square passport-style photograph. He traced a finger over the little boy's solemn face. Rhys had inherited Samira's slightly prominent nose and jet-black wavy hair, but it was impossible to tell if his eyes were his mother's dark brown or Crispin's own sapphire-blue.

He smoothed out the letter on the table.

The fact she'd written from Oxfordshire now made sense because she'd apparently left the army and was putting her skills to good use as a civilian instructor at the Defence Centre for Languages and Culture in Shrivenham.

I'm sorry I didn't tell you when Rhys was born, but I wasn't sure it would be welcome news. My father and I have been estranged since I resigned my commission and I've never confirmed his suspicion that you are Rhys's dad. I hope you will want to know your son even if what we shared is in the past. But you were special to me then and still have a place in my heart, so maybe it is not too late for us to be a family? I hope when we meet we can at least talk about the possibility ...

A trickle of unease ran through him. Back when they were together, Samira told Crispin many times that she loved him and never questioned why he didn't say the same in return. He wanted a relationship with Rhys but needed to make it clear that he'd no interest in anything more than friendship when it came to Samira.

Crispin tucked the picture in his wallet and left the letter folded up on the table. He shrugged on his camouflage jacket and tugged a black wool hat over his messy hair. He'd show the letter to Ashley later before he decided how to reply.

At the bottom of the path, he spotted Ward in the farmhouse doorway with his arm around Nessa bending to kiss little Tristan. It made him think about his own son. Apart from helping Samira out financially, what did she really think he had to offer Rhys?

'Hey mate, you ready to go?' Ward strode across the gravel. 'I've got our instructions.' He waved a list around. 'I'm surprised Lowena's trustin' us on our own.'

'I hope you're a Christmas tree expert because I've never bought one.'

'Never? Didn't you have one growin' up? Every year our folks took me and Ashley out to a nearby farm. Mom picked the tree and Dad cut it. It was a real big deal and we had our picture taken and everythin'.'

'Ours came out of a box.' Crispin recalled the spindly tree they dragged out of the attic every year. 'My sister has an artificial one too. She doesn't like the mess of a live tree.' He chuckled. 'I'm surprised Lowena tolerates it.'

'You forget my sister-in-law is a traditionalist to her bones. Blame Queen Victoria and Charles Dickens for her vision of the perfect Christmas. Luckily Nessa's more laid back.'

'You wouldn't be married to her if she wasn't!'

'True.'

They set off for the Teagues' farm on the other side of Polgarth. One of Polly's endless hoard of stories revolved around Jago Teague having a thing for Nessa long before Ward came on the scene. Supposedly he proposed to Nessa at some point, but she turned him down and they'd remained friends. They planned to hitch Jago's trailer on the back of the truck and load the half a dozen trees they'd been ordered to select, all of which would be planted outside after Christmas.

'While I've got you captive, I've got a favour to ask. How do you feel about joining me and the Wheal Boys on Christmas Eve at the pub?'

'To sing? You've got to be joking.' Crispin's horror made Ward chuckle. They'd chatted recently while they were working on the farm about the traditional songs they both loved, and had even sung a few together out of earshot of anyone else. This bizarre suggestion was something else entirely and simply thinking about it brought him out in a cold sweat.

'I've told the boys about you and they know we're short of time to try to rehearse together, but the two of us can run through them here and if we get to the pub in good time, we'll be fine. I'm only talking about a couple of songs, not the whole set.' Ward's wheedling tone dragged a smile out of Crispin. 'Think about it.'

Crispin was thankful Ward backed off and didn't press him any further while they drove the rest of the way.

Today was only the first of December, still early for most people to think about buying their tree, and mid-week, so they found themselves to be the only customers when they reached the tree farm. They soon selected and chopped down their own trees and loaded up for the drive back.

'Nessa's not home because she's taken Tris to visit one of her friends in St Austell, so I vote we go to Tregereth first. If we're lucky we'll wangle a lunch invitation.' Ward cracked a grin. 'Of course that's assuming the trees meet with Lowena's approval, or it could be bread and water for us.'

Back at the house they parked around the back, and Ward jumped out to bang on the kitchen door.

'Hey ladies, your Christmas tree delivery is here. You wanna come take a look?'

Ashley flung open the door and latched eyes with Crispin, ignoring her brother.

'What's wrong?' Her tight, anxious smile worried him.

'Nothing's wrong, but you've got visitors.'

Crispin's heart stopped when another woman appeared too. 'Samira?' The ruby-red V-neck jumper and slim-fitting black trousers highlighted her familiar hourglass figure, but before today he'd only seen her glossy dark hair loose around her shoulders when they'd shared a bed.

'Crispin! How wonderful to see you again!' She threw her arms open and stepped towards him. A frown knotted her smooth brow when he didn't move.

He'd noticed that Ashley hadn't taken her eyes off them and dreaded to imagine what was going through her mind.

'You didn't ring, so I took the chance and came anyway.'

'I only got your letter this morning.'

'I'm sorry. I thought the post would be faster.' She pulled forward a little boy and Crispin couldn't tear his gaze from the shy child clinging to his mother's legs. 'This is Rhys.'

More than anything he longed to hug his son but was terrified of frightening him. 'Does he know who I am?'

'I've tried to explain but it's a bit confusing.'

He bit back the urge to say that wasn't his fault. There was no point in recriminations now.

'Lowena, do you want to see if these trees meet your approval?' Ward spoke up.

'I'd be delighted.'

The two of them disappeared towards the trailer, and he wasn't sure what to suggest next.

'Why don't we all go inside and I'll put the kettle on?' Ashley offered with a sly smile in his direction. Her ongoing amusement about the British reliance on hot tea was a running joke between them.

'Great idea.'

'I don't suppose Crispin has changed that much since we were together. The British Army runs on tea and he drank gallons every day, even when the temperature nudged forty degrees.'

Samira's throwaway comment made him wince. Crispin would have bridges to repair with Ashley later because he wasn't prepared to lose her. But he couldn't lose his son either. Balancing the two could be his biggest challenge ever.

Ashley fumbled with the teabags and jumped when Crispin's fingers wrapped around her hand.

'I'll make it. Sit down.'

She could hardly say she didn't want to make any more polite conversation with Samira so did as he'd suggested. The woman's exotic beauty and air of entitlement when she talked about Crispin made her feel inadequate. It'd shaken her to the core when the woman turned up an hour ago in a taxi with the gorgeous little boy in tow. No one had been around at Pear Tree Farm when she'd arrived there, and the driver suggested coming to Tregereth because he knew the connection between the two places.

'Are you planning to stay long?' Ashley tried to sound welcoming.

'I thought maybe a few days?' Samira shrugged. 'The students finished their exams yesterday and I'm free until classes restart after the New Year.' Her wide mouth curled into a satisfied smile.

It ripped a hole in her heart to watch Crispin's dark eyes devouring his son while he waited for the tea to brew. She shouldn't condemn Samira for not telling him they were expecting a child together, but it meant he'd missed so much of Rhys's childhood through no fault of his own.

'We need to talk.' Samira ignored the mug he placed in front of her.

'Do you think Rhys would be happy to come outside with me?' Ashley's tentative question earned her a fleeting smile from Crispin. 'We could have a walk around in the garden while you chat.'

'Thank you. That would be helpful.' The woman's forced smile didn't fool her. Samira reached for the boy's black padded anorak on the back of his chair and got him dressed. Rhys didn't say a word but threw Ashley a wary look, his dark blue eyes the eerie mirror image of Crispin's.

She shrugged on her jacket and slipped a chocolate wafer in her pocket. A wave of emotion came close to undoing her when Rhys slipped his small, warm hand in hers. The baby she'd lost would've been a toddler by now and clutching her hand in that same trusting way.

It was a relief to be out in the cold, bright sunshine, and Ashley chatted away to Rhys as they explored. The first time he gave her a shy smile and giggled when a squirrel ran across in front of them, she felt she'd won the lottery. After that they played hide and seek and tag until they were both out of breath. A wide grin identical to Crispin's lit up the little boy's face when she surprised him with the biscuit. 'Shall we go back to your mom and uh …?' She let the rest of the question go. The kid wouldn't think of Crispin as his father. Not yet.

'Okay.'

When Ashley pushed open the kitchen door and Crispin turned around his face radiated anxiety. Samira's expression held an air of triumph. She did her best to smile and tightened her grip on Rhys's hand.

Chapter Sixteen

Crispin knew Ashley's tight smile was a cover for her uncertainty and wished they were alone.

'Look, Mummy. This one's for me to keep.' Rhys ran over to Samira and showed her a pine cone. 'We saw a squirrel too.'

'May I see it?' His son gave him a cautious look then edged closer and offered it to him. 'Did you have fun playing in the garden?'

One solemn nod.

Usually he got on better with kids than adults, but he was tongue-tied around the boy who was his own flesh and blood. Rhys swiped the precious object from him when he offered it back and retreated to the safety of his mother's orbit.

'Crispin, are you going to ask Ashley the favour I mentioned?' Samira nodded at him.

'What do you need? I'll help if I can.'

'Do you think Ward would mind if Samira and Rhys have the attic room for a few days? It's not reserved for guests, is it?' He couldn't blame her for looking dismayed.

'No, we've only booked the main bedrooms for the festival weekends. I'm sure it won't be a problem.'

'That's very kind of you.' Samira looked satisfied. 'You will stay here too, Crispin?'

'Me?' His cheeks burned. 'No, I've got a caravan down at the farm.'

'Ah, what a pity.'

'I've got a lot of work to do so I'd better get on.' The chair legs scraped on the flagstones as he stood up. 'I'll be in and out of the house for a while setting up Christmas trees then we've got to go back down to the farm with the other trees. You've caught us at a busy time.' He smiled at his son. 'Bye, Rhys. Next time I come we'll play.'

'Okay.'

It took him by surprise in a good way when Ashley followed him over to the door and tilted her cheek for a kiss. 'I'll ring you later. It's … complicated.'

'It would be.' That sliver of humour lifted his spirits. 'Off you go. We'll be fine.'

When he stepped outside Ward and Lowena stopped talking, and it didn't take a genius to guess what they'd been chatting about. 'Are we ready to shift trees?'

'Yeah. The boss has selected the four to stay here so we'll start with those.' Ward pointed to the trailer. 'One's for the upstairs landing, another in the drawing room and the biggest in the entrance hall. We'll keep the smallest for the private living room off the kitchen.'

Crispin tossed his jacket in the truck and got to work. By the time they'd fitted the trees into stands and situated them to Lowena's satisfaction, he felt a little easier in his mind.

'Back to the farm?' Ward swiped a hand over his sweaty face. 'My stomach feels like my throat's been cut. How about we grab a couple of pasties at the shop and take them home to eat?'

If they landed in the farmhouse kitchen and Nessa was back, she'd ask a million and one questions. He wasn't up for that but didn't know how to say so.

'On second thoughts, we'll wolf them down in the truck. It'll be quicker.'

'Works for me.' Nothing more needed to be said.

*

'Have you known Crispin long?'

Samira's question made Ashley stop what she was doing. They were sorting through the Christmas ornaments she'd helped Lowena buy in Truro last week. She needed to be careful how she replied because she had no idea how much the other woman knew about the time Crispin spent AWOL from the army. 'We met briefly last year, but we've become much closer over the last couple of months.' Ashley sensed that Samira hoped to rekindle her relationship with Crispin. How he felt about that was the huge elephant-in-the-room question. She wished she could be certain it was the furthest thing from his mind, but Samira wielded a powerful tool in the form of Rhys. The boy's existence changed everything.

Samira cradled a fragile gold ball decorated with intricate red scrollwork in her elegant hands. 'Do you have children?'

'No. I was married briefly but we divorced.'

'Rhys and I have done well on our own since he was born, but I've come to see he needs his father in his life. That's why I reached out to Crispin.' She fixed her dark eyes on Ashley. 'I hope you will encourage him to be involved in raising our son?'

'Of course.'

'Come out and see the tree we've finished in the hall.' Lowena bustled in with Rhys trailing along behind her. 'He's been a huge help – haven't you, dear?' She patted his head. 'He passes the decorations to me and he's very careful. It's lovely having a young one around the house.'

She seized the chance to escape and followed them out. Ashley breathed in the fragrant scent of fresh pine and stared at the magnificent tree whose gold star almost touched the ceiling. The traditional decorations – swoops of shiny dark red ribbon and simple white lights – suited the old house perfectly. 'Oh wow, that's awesome.'

'One down and three to go. Are you tired, Rhys?' It was impossible not to smile when the boy shook his head fiercely at Lowena. 'Good boy. We'll go upstairs. Maybe you two can manage to decorate the small one?' Without waiting for a reply, she whisked Rhys away.

'You know we're only trusted with that particular tree because guests aren't allowed in that space so she'll grit her teeth and tolerate a less than perfect job?' Ashley whispered as soon as Lowena was out of earshot.

'I guessed as much. She would have made a great army officer.' Samira's smile broadened.

'Yeah, I can see that.'

They laughed together, and Ashley found herself wondering if she was being unfair to demonise the other woman. Could she honestly blame Samira for wanting to give her son the sort of upbringing she'd had herself and valued? That was a conversation she needed to have with Crispin later and she already dreaded it.

He couldn't work out where the loud banging was coming from. Crispin had flopped on the bed after he finished work to rest his eyes for a few minutes but must have fallen asleep. The noise shifted from the caravan door to his bedroom window.

'You gonna let me in?' Ashley peered in through a gap in the curtains.

'The door's open.' He dragged himself off the bed and was in the middle of pulling pine needles out of his hair when she strolled in.

'Lowena's fixin' dinner for six o'clock and I've been sent to get you.'

Crispin opened his arms to hug her, but she stepped out of reach without a smile so he dropped them away again. 'That's fine but I need to shower and change,' he said.

'Yeah, I can see that – but there's somethin' I need to say first.' A shadow crossed her face. 'I've been doin' a lot of thinkin' this afternoon. You've got a lot goin' on right now and your priority is to sort things out with Samira. You don't need the complication of … us in addition to everything else.'

'Are you dumping me?' He couldn't believe what he was hearing.

'No! I'm just suggesting we put things on hold for now. I don't want to but it makes sense, and if you're honest you'll admit I'm right.' Ashley's anguished voice tore at him.

'In case I didn't make myself clear, I've no interest in being with Samira again … that way.' His face heated. 'Don't you think I can be a good father to Rhys and … have a relationship with you at the same time?' He'd almost made the mistake of spelling out his growing feelings for her more specifically but that would be abysmal timing. 'Forget it. I'm too tired to think straight right now, so I probably don't know what I'm saying. I'll skip dinner tonight, but will you tell Samira and Rhys I'll be up to see them tomorrow?'

'Yeah, of course. Is that it?'

What more does she want from me? Crispin wondered. He watched her eyes turn glassy with tears but made no attempt to comfort her. With all the self-control he could muster, he held the same rigid stance until she slammed the door on her way out. Then he slumped back on the bed and dropped his head in his hands.

Chapter Seventeen

Despite the emptiness in her heart, Ashley smiled at the scene in front of her. For this first day of "Christmas, Cornish Style" the air carried a suitably festive cold bite, the sky was a stunning clear blue and the sun hadn't stopped shining. With a little over three weeks to go until Christmas, they'd apparently timed it perfectly to pull in the crowds. It'd been non-stop since they opened at ten this morning, and she was about run ragged trying to make sure the food and craft vendors had everything they needed. She'd heard that things were equally busy down at the farm and most of the visitors she'd spoken to were checking out both venues.

'I've settled Josh and Linda Mason in the Bluebell Room, so that's all our overnight guests here now.' Lowena brandished her clipboard like a deadly weapon.

'Awesome.'

'Ward rang a minute ago to say they need more leaflets at the farm to hand out – the ones with all the vendors listed? Would you mind running some down?'

'I could but—'

'But nothing. I've got other things to do.' Her friend's sharp eyes bored into her.

'Fine. I'll go.'

'Good girl.'

She almost sniped at Lowena for patronising her, but it wasn't her fault that Ashley's love life had gone down the tubes.

'I'm not unsympathetic my dear, just practical. You're not the only one who's had hard lessons to learn.'

A wave of guilt swept through her. Lowena's ex-husband

destroyed his almost twenty-year marriage because he was flattered by a young woman's attention, and by the time it petered out and he discovered he wanted his old life back, it was too late. His son wanted little to do with him and Lowena had sloughed off her bitterness and found an outlet for her considerable skills in her new job. Her friend was the poster child for not looking back.

A new resolve surged through her. She would get through this. She went inside to grab a pile of leaflets then headed down the road.

A small group of Salvation Army members were gathered in front of the farmhouse singing 'God Rest Ye Merry Gentlemen' and she dug some money out her wallet to put in their collection box. Inviting them was Nessa's idea – in part to add to the festive atmosphere but also because they were a favourite of her late father.

She couldn't see Ward straight away, but before she had a chance to pull out her mobile to call him, Ashley froze. The crowds of people swarming around left her no choice but to stay put and it was inevitable that Crispin would spot her any second now. He was striding her way, wearing Dickensian-style work clothes with the colourful scarf she'd sewn knotted around his neck. He'd hoisted Rhys out of the crowd up on his shoulders and Samira's hand was linked through one of his arms.

The last three days had been some of the worst ever. She'd been determined not to give Samira any cause for complaint so she managed to plaster on a smile whenever Crispin snatched time away from work to turn up at Tregereth and spend time with his son. Rhys was starting to open up to his newly-discovered father, and it was bittersweet to watch them play and laugh together. Yesterday she told herself she'd definitely made the right choice when she overheard the little boy call him "Daddy", but then she caught the naked sadness written all over Crispin's face when he glanced Ashley's way and her resolve had crumbled.

'Look what I have!' Rhys tumbled down from Crispin's arms and ran over to her. 'It's a Christmas teddy bear.' He thrust the garish red stuffed animal in her hands. It sported a green bow around its neck and had the words *Ho Ho Ho* embroidered on its chest. 'My daddy won it for me. He knocked a Christmas pudding off a stick.'

'That's awesome.' She conjured up her brightest smile. 'Are you havin' a good time?'

'Oh yes.' Samira chipped in. 'You've done an incredible job with this festival. I love all of the artisan crafts and managed to buy most of my Christmas presents already.'

'I'm pleased to hear it.'

'You've all made us so welcome. I've never been to Cornwall before, but everyone is so friendly – I can see why Crispin chose to settle here. Being here makes me wonder if I should reconsider my job and where we live. Bringing Rhys up in the countryside would be so much healthier.'

'It's something to think about.' She blinked away a rush of tears. 'I have to go.' She held up the large brown envelope. 'If I don't deliver these leaflets to Ward, I'll be in trouble with "she-who-must-be-obeyed".'

She'd done the stupidest thing on the planet and was paying the price.

The hum of the crowd around him. Rhys's shrill laughter. Samira's contented smile. Everything faded away except for the pure, unadulterated longing etched into Ashley's face.

She couldn't hide her feelings and Crispin guessed he was doing a similarly lousy job. With her blonde hair curled up around the soft brim of a dark green velvet hat she looked like Santa's favourite elf, and as Crispin's hand strayed unconsciously to his scarf a flicker of her smile returned.

'You'll find Ward up in the top field covering for me at the hot cider stand.'

'How on earth did you get roped into doin' that? I thought you provided physical labour only and stayed well away from people?'

'Everyone's mucking in. We're busier than expected. That's good, right?'

'Yeah, everything's good.'

The wobble in her voice betrayed the obvious lie. For a second, he was stupid enough to wonder how they got to this place but Crispin knew the answer lay in the dark-eyed woman resting her hand on his arm and the smiling little boy with his own dark blue eyes.

'I really do need to go. Have fun.' Ashley left an awkward silence behind her.

'I'm hungry.' Rhys tugged at his leg.

'We'll go get something.' He ruffled his son's head.

'You should go back to work. We'll be okay.' Samira's quiet assurance made him feel guilty.

'It's not a problem. Ward told me not to hurry. I hear there's a lady selling mince pies in the walled garden.' Crispin smiled at Rhys. 'And another with Christmas biscuits in all sorts of fancy shapes, like snowmen and reindeer. Does that sound good?'

'Ooh! Yes please, Daddy.'

Every time the little boy called him that it tightened his son's hold on his heart. They walked towards the garden and he debated how to ask about the bombshell Samira had just dropped. 'Are you seriously considering giving up your job? You'll struggle to find something else to use your experience and skills if you're stuck out in the countryside.'

'You don't think Rhys would benefit?'

It would be a lie if he said no, but encouraging her could steer him towards something he didn't want and saw plainly now wouldn't work. 'What about your family? Aren't they all in the south-east?'

'We don't see much of them. My parents are disappointed in me.' He remembered one night in Kabul she'd confided that her father had groomed her for command, determined she would be the first female four-star general. 'Daddy was horrified when I resigned from the army. He said it was totally unnecessary and that everyone made mistakes.' She grimaced. 'He assured me all the top officers had skeletons in their closets and that an unplanned baby needn't ruin my career.' Her eyes hardened. 'I refused to have Rhys referred to as a mistake. He's my family now and I'm fine with that.'

'Well, in that case, it's something to think about.' Of course he absolutely wanted what was best for his son, but his old feelings for Samira couldn't be recreated and anything less wouldn't be fair to either of them.

'Yes, it is.' The challenge was unmistakeable.

'Time for mince pies.' He swept his son back up in his arms. 'Come on, let's beat your mum to the food.' The boy's giggles grew louder when he dodged around the other people to reach the queue for mince pies.

How was he going to convince Ashley that he could be a good father to Rhys and still have the chance to make a life with her?

Chapter Eighteen

Crispin straightened up and rubbed both hands over his sore back. He'd spent the whole day clearing up from the weekend and had finally finished shifting the stalls back into the shed. On Friday, they'd be dragged back out again for the second of the Christmas themed weekends. Apart from the idea of moving to the countryside, Samira had dropped another possibility on him yesterday that'd been on his mind ever since.

'How would you feel if we stayed here to celebrate Christmas with you?'

He'd mumbled something about being busy with work and not liking to take advantage of Ward's generosity but in the end had agreed to ask yet another favour.

'All right, mate?' Ward ambled in with an armful of signs and stacked them in the corner.

'I've been better.'

His friend gave him a long stare. 'Bit of a shake-up, Samira and little Rhys arriving like that. It's knocked you for six.'

'Yep, but I promise I'm not messing Ashley around.'

'I believe you. She's stubborn, right?' Ward chuckled. 'Probably insisted on cooling things between the pair of you so you could concentrate on sorting things out?'

His face burned. The sibling thing was a killer. No one understood him as well as Rhonda either. They didn't see each other often or stay in touch like they should, but the connection never went away.

'It explains why she's goin' around like a bear with a sore head. You're bloody good for each other, and if the

111

two of you screw this up, you'll have a whole bunch of folk to reckon with. Me. Nessa. Jack. Polly.' He counted them off on his fingers. 'Not forgetting Lowena.' Ward rolled his eyes. 'My sister-in-law could put the fear of God into Attila the Hun so you won't stand a chance.'

'You wouldn't prefer someone less ... complicated for her?' That earned him a wry smile.

'For a start, she'd rip me a new one if I tried to tell her *who* I thought she should hook up with, and anyway, my sister's not exactly straightforward now, is she?'

'I suppose.' Crispin felt awkward. 'I've another favour to ask.' He threw Samira's request out there.

'If it's what you want, of course she's welcome to stay.'

'I'd love to spend Christmas with the boy, but she'll have to understand that I ... well, me and Ashley ... you know.'

'Yeah, I know.' Ward's eyes gleamed. 'While we're talkin' about the holidays, have you thought anymore about Christmas Eve?'

'Uh, not really.'

'We could run through the couple of songs I've got in mind one evening this week? Might help you decide. After that, if you're not interested, I'll back off. I promise.'

'Okay I suppose we could.' His reluctant agreement made Ward grin. 'If it's all right with you, I'll get cleaned up now and go to Tregereth.'

'Good idea. Let Samira know where she stands and plead your case with Ashley. It's best you sort things before our folks arrive in another ten days or so.' The broad smile disappeared. 'Mom in particular still feels bad about the fact she didn't see what a jerk Bunny was. Trust me, you're a massive improvement.'

Would the Spencers really welcome a disgraced army veteran who lives in a caravan and works as an odd-job man? he wondered.

'Best of luck, and let us know how you get on.'

'Cheers.' If his nerve held, he'd be good.

Cornwall's winter weather usually leaned towards mild and damp, but he relished the crisp, cold air and bright blue skies they'd been treated to recently. It made the stroll up the road a pleasure rather than a drudge. Out of nowhere Chalky White came to mind, and he wondered if the young marine was still hunkered down at the same campsite where they'd met. It would be a cheerless spot to spend the winter, and despite Ashley's assurance that there was nothing else he could have done, the nagging feeling that he'd failed the young man wouldn't go away.

'Look who I found lurking outside taking his dirty boots off.' Lowena waved a hand over Crispin like a magician conjuring up a live rabbit from his hat and shooed him into the kitchen. 'Tea?' She poured a mug for him without waiting for an answer. 'Sit down.'

'Do you like fish fingers, Daddy?' Rhys stabbed one off his plate and waved it around.

'I certainly do.'

'I thought I heard your voice. I'd know that accent anywhere.' Ashley's honeyed drawl made him sit up straighter.

Crispin did his level best not to gawk. 'Someone's in the Christmas spirit.' Her cheery red sweatshirt was decorated with a sequined Christmas tree and a couple of prancing reindeer. Out of the corner of his eye, he noticed Samira give them both a penetrating stare.

'Everything else was in the laundry hamper.' She stuck her hands on her slender hips and did a model-like twirl. 'Believe it or not, I bought this on the church craft stall last weekend. One of the women in Lowena's old lunch club makes them. There's only so many days you can wear holiday designs, so I might as well make the most of it.'

'Absolutely.' He forced his attention back at Samira. 'I came with good news. Ward's more than happy for you to stay.'

'And you are too?'

'Of course.' The full answer, telling her everything that needed to be said, should be explained in private, although he wasn't sure how to manage that yet.

'Rhys, would you like to help me collect some more pine cones to spray for our Christmas decorations?' Lowena plucked a wicker basket off the counter.

'I'll come too.' Ashley's awkward smile didn't fool him, but he could hardly ask her to stay.

Alone with Samira, he wasn't sure where to start but went for the easy bit. 'I'm really glad you can stay longer so I can spend more time with Rhys. He's an amazing boy and you've done an incredible job raising him with so little help from anyone else and certainly none from me.'

'You would've done, if I'd told you about him.'

'Would I?' Crispin managed a fleeting smile. 'It's doubtful. I was a mess back then. I wouldn't have been much use.'

'I wasn't much better.' Samira lowered her gaze so he couldn't read her expression. 'You were the only bright light in the whole damn mess we were mired in.' She plucked at the sleeve of her black jumper. 'I'm not sure you or anyone appreciated how hard it was for me. Apart from my mother teaching me the language, I'd never really identified with that side of my heritage. Mum had never even been to Afghanistan. Every day I dealt with a ton of guilt that dragged me down and made it tough to do my job.' A wobbly smile lifted the straight set of her mouth. 'Having Rhys saved me so I have no regrets.'

'I'm relieved to hear it.' Crispin instinctively reached over to cradle her hands.

'Do you think if we'd met in different circumstances, we might've …?' She glanced back up and her dark eyes bored into him. 'Is it too late? We could make a good life together. A real family for our son.' Samira lowered her voice to a husky whisper. 'Maybe have another baby?'

He pulled his hands back. 'No. I'm sorry. That's not going to happen.' She recoiled as though he'd slapped her. 'I want to be a father to Rhys, see him as much as I can and be there to help raise him … but that's it.'

'Would your answer be different if Ashley wasn't around?'

'I don't think so, but I can't be certain.' That was the frankest he could be. 'But she is and I care for her very much, and I'm hopeful we might have a future together so it's beside the point. We're both different people now. We've got our acts together and made fresh starts.'

'I think it's time we tracked down our pine cone hunters.' Samira stood up and grabbed a Cornish tartan cape from the back of the chair. She wrapped it around her narrow shoulders. 'Do you like it? I thought I should buy something to celebrate your adopted part of the world.'

Crispin was thrown. Samira's brittle smile unnerved him,

but he couldn't decide if he was reading too much into her seemingly casual acceptance. Ashley would warn him to trust his gut so that's what he'd do. Watching his back was never a bad idea.

Chapter Nineteen

If she didn't hurry, she'd be late and Crispin might get the wrong idea. He'd texted and asked her to come down to the farm after they both finished work so they could talk. It would be the first chance they'd had since yesterday. Ashley swung through the kitchen to find her handbag and was surprised to find Samira in the middle of making coffee.

'Are you going out?' Samira shook her head. 'Sorry, that's none of my business.'

'Don't be.' She shrugged on her dark green coat and wrapped the Cornish tartan scarf around her neck. 'Yes, I'm off to see Crispin.'

'I'm glad the two of you are not being silly because of me any longer. Crispin and I cleared the air. Everything is good.'

'I'm pleased.' Despite Samira's bright, friendly manner, something struck her as a little off about the woman. It was as though she was biding her time about something.

'I'll see you later, I expect … at some point.'

Samira's coy look grated on Ashley but she dredged up a smile before making her escape.

Following Lowena's instructions, the farmhouse had been decked out in full Christmas mode before the first of the festival weekends, so hundreds of white lights now sparkled along the roofline and fresh holly wreaths set off with wide red velvet bows hung on all the windows. She was half way up the path towards "Mr Blue Sky" when she heard raised voices coming from Polly and Jack's pink camper. Next thing, a middle-aged man she didn't recognise

117

stomped out then turned around to shout something else before he stalked off and swept down past her without speaking, his face like thunder. She spotted Crispin hovering on his top step with a worried frown etched into his face.

'Who was that?'

'That's Julian Bullen. Polly and Jack's nephew.'

She remembered Ward telling her about the friction their nephew caused when he first visited and forced the story about the baby boy that the couple lost to become public knowledge.

'I don't know what's up but I think I should find out. Are you coming?' He leapt down and ran over.

'Do you think they'll want me sticking my nose in?'

'Why not? We're their friends.'

'Could you make out what was goin' on?'

'Not really.'

She suppressed a bubble of laughter when his freshly shaved cheeks turned pink and he admitted he'd been popping his head out of the door at regular intervals to watch for her.

'I saw Julian arrive and Jack let him in, but next thing they were back outside and Polly was screeching at them. All I could catch was something about Birmingham and family.'

'That's not good. Come on then.'

Jack flung open the door before they could knock. 'You might as well come in. I told Polly you'd be up.'

'We don't want to interfere—'

'Yeah, we do.' Ashley stopped Crispin's attempt to apologise. 'We're your friends.'

'I suppose the walls have ears as usual.' Polly was

hunched over the kitchen table, and when she glanced up her eyes were red-rimmed and swollen.

'Y'all were screaming the place down. We didn't need a hearing aid.'

'Sit down.' Jack sounded weary. 'Julian brought bad news from Polly's family back in Birmingham. Her sister Meg, that's Julian's mum, is really poorly and wants to see Polly before she … uh … but we don't feel we can go.'

'Were you and Meg close?' Ashley's question eradicated the last dregs of colour from Polly's face but her friend's mouth stayed in a tight, silent line. 'If you were then I don't see you've got a choice. I'd never forgive myself if it was Ward and I stayed away.'

'Even if he'd called you a wicked person who deserved to burn in hell?' Polly rounded on her.

'I'm guessin' Julian said she's sorry for that now?'

'Yes. That was in the message he brought from his dad,' Jack explained.

'If you're so torn up about Meg, you can go see her on your own,' Polly yelled at him and stormed out, slamming the door behind her hard enough that it bounced off the wall.

'Do you want me to go after her?'

Jack shook his head. 'Let her walk it off. She feels guilty, you see. Meg wasn't the only one who said things she shouldn't have. It was the morning after we lost little Danny and tempers were running high.' He shrugged. 'If we'd stayed a bit longer, I expect we'd have made up, but the longer things drift on the harder it is to put them right.'

'But if you don't go now, it could be too late and how's that gonna make you feel?' She purposely homed in on the one thing no-one could dispute.

'Worse.'

Ashley pressed her point home. 'Call Polly's bluff. Tell the family you're coming and make your plans. I bet you anythin' she goes along with you when the time comes.'

'You think so?' Jack sounded dubious.

'I'm sure of it.' Ashley caught Crispin's frown. Had she overstepped the mark? The last thing she wanted was to throw a wrench in the Greens' marriage.

'Good luck.' Crispin pushed his chair back. 'Let us know if you need anything.' He gently steered her outside.

'Okay, let me have it,' she said, when they were a safe distance so that Jack couldn't hear.

'What?'

'You think I shouldn't have stuck my oar in.'

'I wouldn't say that.'

'But?' Her persistence made him smile. 'I might've been a bit ... Lowena-ish?'

'Is that even a word?'

'Does it matter? Should I go back and apologise or—'

'Leave it. They'll sort things out and be fine. They're solid.'

'Do you think we could be too?' Ashley's question made his eyes darken.

'Yeah.' Crispin gave her a rueful smile. 'I think we've got some talking to do first though, don't you?'

'Do you want to tell me what Samira said? Or I can run through everything we talked about. Your choice.' Her provocative look told him to hurry up. 'She said you'd cleared the air and everything was good.'

'But?'

'I wasn't convinced.'

You're right not to be, he thought. Crispin knew if he held anything back now, they were doomed. 'I told her categorically that I want to be a father to Rhys, see as much of him as I can and help Samira raise him, but that any idea of us being a couple again wasn't happening.' He swallowed hard. 'When she asked if my answer would've been different if you weren't around, I said that was irrelevant because I care deeply for you.' Her eyes widened. Crispin wished he was the sort of man who could talk about his feelings and emotions without turning into a block of wood. 'I can cope with her, but I'm more concerned about your parents. They'll be here soon and I'm afraid they won't think I'm good enough for you.' His palms started to sweat and the back of his neck prickled.

'How old am I?' Ashley's voice took on a new harder edge.

'I'm not sure. Is this some sort of test? Late twenties?'

'I turned thirty earlier this year. Yeah, I want my folks to see what a good guy you are but I'm not their little girl any longer. At the end of the day, you'll either be my choice or you won't. Right now, I'd say you are … but it's early days.'

He picked over her answer in his head and came to the conclusion it was generally positive.

'Is there anything else we *have* to talk about because I think there are other things we might rather do?' Even he could recognise an invitation spelled out that clearly. 'You're allowed to speak.'

'I'm trying.' The thick rasp in his voice brought out her wicked smile.

Ashley dragged him to her. 'Come on.'

In the bedroom, she stripped down to her delicate white lace underwear and gave him a provocative smile. Crispin slipped the thin bra straps over her shoulders, exposing her to his stroking fingers. 'Very pretty.' He wrung out every last drop of self-control to keep from rushing and finally got her naked.

'My turn,' she purred.

He tried counting back from a hundred in his head but around seventy was forced to push her hands away and wriggle out of the rest of his clothes. 'I've waited long enough.'

'Uh, we have done this before in case you've forgotten.'

'As if I could do that. What I'm trying to say is that I never thought I'd be in this place in my life.' If he was too honest about his hopes for a future with Ashley, it might frighten her off. 'Come to bed.'

'If you insist.'

'Oh, I do.'

Chapter Twenty

'And what are you smirking about, as if I didn't know?' Lowena strode into the kitchen. 'Your hero is here with more folding chairs for the tea tent. I'll finish up the mince pies if you don't mind helping him out?'

'I suppose I could.' Another smile bubbled up inside Ashley; simply thinking about the last three nights that they'd spent together since their reconciliation made her grin at inopportune moments. 'Where are Samira and Rhys by the way? I haven't seen them since breakfast.'

'She volunteered to work a shift on the Whack-an-Elf game. I think it's a travesty of Christmas, but people can't seem to get enough of it.'

'The Society for the Protection of Elves haven't protested yet so don't get your knickers in a twist.' She pointed to a stainless-steel baking tray covered with neat rows of mince pies. 'Those are ready to go in the oven.' For someone who'd never heard of the popular Christmas delicacies until last year, she was proud of how fast she could knock them out now. Ashley washed her hands and flung on her favourite dark green coat, wrapped the Cornish tartan scarf around her neck and added the green velvet beret she'd bought on one of the stalls the previous weekend.

Her heart raced when she peeked out of the kitchen window and spotted Crispin heading towards the tea tent. He was hauling chairs off the truck in his shirtsleeves, giving her a great view of his brawny forearms.

She hurried out to catch up with him. 'I've been sent to help.'

'Reluctant, were you?' He strolled over and swooped in for a kiss. 'Didn't think so.'

'Sure of yourself, are we?'

Crispin's eyes turned wary. 'Today's the big day. What time do your parents get into Truro?'

'About half past four. Ward's goin' to pick them up. There's no need to be nervous.' They both knew that wasn't completely true. Her mum and dad weren't snobs, and they couldn't care less if she hooked up with a heart surgeon or a street sweeper, but they'd seen her badly hurt by one man so would naturally be cautious.

'Do you still want me to come here for dinner tomorrow?'

Ward had taken first dibs on their parents tonight so they could get to know their grandson. 'Yeah, of course I do. Lowena's offered to take Samira and Rhys to see the Christmas lights in Truro and shop at the market so it'll just be the four of us.'

'Have you told your parents about them?' Worry lines furrowed his brow.

'No, I thought it would be better to explain face to face. Ward and Nessa have promised not to say anything.'

'I suppose that's best.' Crispin didn't sound convinced. 'I'd better get on now or I won't have a job and that'll be another black mark against me.'

'My daddy isn't gonna ask to see your bank statements.'

He frowned at the darkening sky. 'The weather forecast is lousy for the rest of the weekend. We're in for showers later and it's turning a lot colder overnight. Tomorrow could be a wash out.'

Ashley didn't miss his subtle change of subject. 'It was

always a gamble. We'll cope. Let's get these chairs sorted before hundreds of people start to roll in.'

'Ever the optimist.'

'I've gotta be around you.'

Normally the steady beat of rain on the caravan roof lulled him into a deep sleep, but it hadn't worked last night. He'd laid there for hours fretting, which was idiotic. All he could do was lay out the facts to Ashley's parents and hope they accepted him, warts and all.

On mornings like this he couldn't be bothered to trail down to the shower block, so Crispin squeezed into his miniature bathroom and shifted his large body around under the hot water to slough off the worst of his lethargy. He abandoned the idea of breakfast and made do with a mug of strong tea gulped down at the kitchen window. Ashley would tell him off if she caught him without the obligatory Cornish tartan scarf around his neck so he dutifully tied it on, although it wasn't visible once he threw on his oilskin cape and yanked up the hood. His work boots were still damp after yesterday's rain so he pulled on his wellies instead and set off. The morning's first task was to do a thorough check around the farm before the vendors arrived. He'd make sure everything was in place then trek up to Tregereth and repeat the process there. If he was lucky that might snag him a few minutes alone with Ashley and the chance to steal a few kisses.

He surveyed the sight in front of him and groaned. This wasn't good. The gravel path leading to the shepherd's huts had basically washed away in the night and the field was little more than a sea of mud. If he went down to give

Ward a heads up about the damage, it could lead to an impromptu meeting with Ashley's parents. There were still a couple of hours before the vendors were allowed in so he'd have a go at fixing it by himself.

Crispin slogged away, dragging old planks of wood from the barn to make temporary paths. He picked up his pace but, out of nowhere, the muddy ground got the better of him and he lost his footing. He dropped the board he was carrying and slammed his foot down to regain his balance. A split-second too late he spotted a long nail sticking up out of the wood and a sharp pain shot up through his leg. Two army rules that should have been ingrained in his stubborn brain came back to haunt him. *Check your equipment. Wear the right uniform.* He should have been wearing his heavy-duty work boots and been paying closer attention.

It'd be a waste of time to shout for help because no one else was outside yet and his mobile was still plugged in by his bedside table. Crispin eked out a wry smile. His old army mates would call him out for being a wimp, only they wouldn't phrase it that kindly. He'd endured a damn sight worse in the past and kept on fighting – literally – through a broken arm and a gunshot in the thigh. Crispin gritted his teeth, steadied his good foot on the board, and pulled.

'Oh my God, what on earth have you done?'

Nessa's horrified screech made him almost topple over.

'I got a nail in my foot, that's all. It's out now. I'll clean it up, stick a plaster on and it'll be good.'

Behind her an older couple were walking along with Ward, and it didn't take a genius to guess who they were. The petite blonde carrying Tristan was the spitting image of Ashley and the craggy grey-haired man was his son in another thirty years.

'The rain's stopped at last so we thought we'd have a bit of fresh air. What's up?' The older man's gaze narrowed on Crispin.

'I got a nail in my foot. It's not a big deal.'

'Let me take a look. I was a nurse.' Mrs Spencer approached him with the same determined look he'd seen multiple times on her daughter's face. 'Let's get inside the barn.'

Next thing he was inside and sitting down with his boot and socks removed. She crouched down and examined him with deft hands. 'You need to see a doctor. They'll clean it properly, give you a tetanus shot and some antibiotics.'

'Dr Thomas isn't in his surgery at weekends so I'd recommend going to the minor injury unit at the St Austell community hospital rather than all the way to Truro.' Nessa frowned. 'What were you doing anyway?'

He rattled off the story and their recriminations sent a wave of tiredness sweeping through him. 'Stick me in a taxi and I'll be fine.'

'I've already texted Ash and she's on the way.' Ward chipped in. 'She'll take you.'

'No one's introduced us.' Ashley's mother stuck out her hand. 'I'm Fiona Spencer. You must be—'

'Daddy, Daddy! I walked all the way down the big road with Mummy.' Rhys pelted in through the barn and raced towards him. 'We're helping Uncle Jack with the games today. He's not my real uncle but he told me to call him Uncle Jack.' His son suddenly stopped talking and stared at Crispin's bare outstretched foot. 'Where's your boot?'

'I did something silly and got a nail stuck in my foot but it's gone now.'

Rhys's face fell. 'Oh, I wanted to see it.'

'There you are!' Samira ran in and swept their son up in her arms. 'I told you not to run off. That's very naughty.' Crispin watched her become aware of the jostle of people around them. 'Are you all right?'

'I'm fine.' He sighed and briefly told her what was going on. 'We'll get out of the way.'

Crispin could swear he caught a hint of pleasure in her dark eyes before she walked out carrying the protesting little boy just as Ashley came hurrying in.

'Are you all right?' Ashley was panting for breath and pale as a ghost. She jerked to a halt and her anxious gaze flitted around them all. 'Oh! Mom, Dad?'

'Your mother's been kind enough to play Florence Nightingale for me.' He watched the expression on her face change as her brain raced.

'Give us both a quick hug sweetheart, then you can run along and get this young man to the doctor and we'll talk properly over dinner later.' Fiona put a clear end to the conversation. *For now.*

Crispin levered himself off the chair and brushed off Ashley's attempt to hold onto his arm. They should have been forthright with her parents to start with. This was all his fault.

Ashley pulled her father to one side and lowered her voice. 'I'll explain all about Rhys, Crispin's little boy, later. I promise you Crispin's a great guy.' Her face burned.

'Do what your mother says and go get his foot seen to.'

Frustration gnawed at her, but she knew there'd be plenty

of time to argue her case later. She switched her attention back to Crispin. 'Are you all set? I borrowed Lowena's car.'

'Do you know where the hospital is?'

Ashley threw him a withering glance. 'Of course I know. I'm almost a local now. Come on.' She slipped her arm through his so he could lean on her as they walked – or in his case hopped – outside.

'I'm sorry I didn't speak up back there. I was rattled.'

'Can't imagine why.'

'Yeah right.'

She thought it best to leave the conversation alone and clicked the key fob to open the passenger door. Crispin eased himself in and leaned his head against the window. Neither of them spoke as they drove through the village and made the short journey to St Austell. She took her time parking because it wouldn't do to return a scratched car. They linked arms again and followed the signs for the clinic. Ashley settled in the waiting room while he approached the receptionist's window and soon he'd limped back to join her.

'It could be a while but they'll fit me in.' He took the seat next to her. 'Your parents are going to think I'm a right shit now.'

'Are you ashamed of Rhys?' Crispin looked shocked. 'No? I didn't think so and I'm not either. Lots of people have previous relationships, partners, children … marriages.' She put special emphasis on the last word. 'We're not kids. Mom and Dad will understand. I'll make it clear I was the one who put off telling them, not you.' Ashley rested her head on his shoulder until a young nurse called his name and Crispin lumbered to his feet. 'Good luck.'

The brief hesitation before he smiled and nodded told her

it'd been on the tip of his tongue to chide her for making a fuss. One day she'd get him used to being cared for. By the time she'd chatted to a young mum with a rambunctious toddler and skimmed the out-of-date magazines, Crispin hobbled back out to join her.

'All set?'

'Yep, I'm patched up and I've a prescription for antibiotics to take. The nurse said there's a chemist inside the supermarket down the road so we can call in there if it's okay with you? Soon as we're done there, we need to get back to work. The festival won't run itself.'

'No problem.'

Back out in the car, she leaned across and kissed him. 'That's for being a big, brave boy.'

'So, if I step on a whole box of nails you'll make it all better in bed tonight?'

'Let's see how things go with my folks first.' She realised how bad that sounded as the words flew out. 'I don't mean they're goin' to change my mind about you—'

'I know that, you silly woman.' Crispin's smile faded a few notches. 'But they're important to you.'

'It's gonna be fine.' Before he could argue any more, she started the car. 'The weather's improving.'

Crispin peered out of the window. 'If we're lucky that patch of blue sky over to the west is headed our way. When we get back to Polgarth you can drop me outside the farm.' He slid her a smile. 'I'll be up later if you need any heavy muscle jobs done.'

'I'm sure I can find something.'

That set them off laughing and her spirits lifted. Surely nothing could shake what they had?

Chapter Twenty-One

Crispin hauled a tarpaulin over the last stall and pegged it to the ground. That was everything covered up ready for tomorrow.

'You're not bailin' on my sister I hope? Dinner with my folks?' Ward set down the black plastic rubbish bags he was hauling to the bins.

'Why'd you say that?'

'You've got your martyr face on.'

'Didn't know I had one.'

'You don't fool me.' His friend's eyes narrowed. 'If you let her down, you'll have me to reckon with. Go get yourself cleaned up and give her some moral support before I bring mom and dad up.'

'Yes, boss.' Crispin flipped a mock salute.

Back in the seclusion of "Mr Blue Sky", he flopped on the sofa and propped up his sore foot. It was time to take another of his antibiotics and he also needed to take another shower, but that would involve wrapping a plastic bag over his foot and he was too exhausted.

'Get your ass out here.'

Ward's angry voice penetrated his fuzzy head and he hobbled over to open the door. 'What's up?' His friend stood on the top step glowering.

'I've got my frantic sister on the phone wondering where the hell you are?'

'Why?'

'Because it's bloody well seven o'clock and they're

waitin' dinner on you. People bein' late riles up my mom no end. Not a good way to kick things off, is it?'

'Hell, I'm sorry.' Crispin shoved a hand through his tangled hair. 'Must've fallen asleep.'

'It's been a long day and I'd take a guess your foot hurts?' Sympathy sneaked into his voice.

'It's been better.'

'I'll call Ashley and put in a good word for you.' Ward clapped a hand on his shoulder. 'Come down when you're ready and I'll run you up in the truck. I should've checked you were there when I dropped Mom and Dad off.'

'Don't beat yourself up. That's my job.' He managed a faint smile.

After an awkward shower, he dragged on a pair of black trousers and a grey jumper. Forcing his foot into a proper shoe made it throb but wearing his dirty work boots wasn't an option. Crispin limped down the path to find Nessa hovering outside her front door.

'Come here so I can see you.'

'Don't give the poor guy any more grief; he's in enough trouble already.' Ward swept a swift, assessing glance over Crispin before Nessa did the same. 'He'll do.'

'Have you both finished examining me like I'm a prize pig?'

Nessa chuckled. 'One who's off to slaughter.' She whipped out a Christmas gift bag from behind her back. 'You bought this fine red wine because it pairs well with the *Boeuf Bourguignon* you'd heard Lowena was making.'

'Thanks. You're the best.'

'Yeah, she is – and don't you ever forget it.' Ward hustled him towards the truck.

In the army he'd trained and prepared for anything that might be thrown his way, but right now Crispin felt like a goldfish about to be fed to a tank of hungry sharks.

For the first time in hours, Ashley relaxed as she listened to Crispin and her father chuckling together over an amusing story from his army days. She'd been worried when he hadn't turned up on time, and when he'd arrived he'd looked so wary and vulnerable. Thankfully she'd overruled Lowena for once and insisted they eat in the kitchen. They needed warmth and comfort tonight, not the magnificence of the elegant dining room with its massive Christmas tree, beautifully decorated fireplace with rows of red candles and fresh greenery, not to mention the newly installed glittering chandelier.

'Is everyone ready for dessert … or pudding, whatever you want to call it?' She lifted over a glazed red pie dish she'd bought at one of the festival stalls and showed off the shimmering tart. 'I can't claim the credit for this either, I'm afraid. It's all down to Lowena. She made this fancy *tarte tatin* using the last of Nessa's fresh pears. I'm informed they're in a caramel sauce with suitably festive spices. You've got to taste this clotted cream with it too.' She added a heaped glass bowl to the table. 'It's the local speciality.'

'If you don't mind, I'd rather wait a bit.' Crispin sounded tentative. 'I'd prefer to clear the air on a few things.'

'Sure.' She sunk back down next to him and reached for his hand under the table. Ashley noticed her mother blink away tears as he spelled out the harsh details of his time in the army, his relationship with Samira and the struggles

133

he faced afterwards. *Could I love this man any more than I do in this moment?* she wondered. It was the first time she'd dared to acknowledge how she'd come to feel about Crispin and her spirits soared.

'You did a damn fine job, son, 'til you couldn't any longer. There's no shame in that.' Her father's quiet observation brought a touch of colour back to Crispin's taut features.

'Todd's speakin' for us both.' Her mother beamed at them. 'The pair of you seem good together and we want to meet your little boy properly, and Samira of course.'

'Thank you for understanding.' Crispin's heavy-lidded eyes bored into her. 'Time for pudding, I think. I'll help you.'

'Yeah, thanks.'

By the time everyone was served and they dived into the mouth-watering tart, it struck her that the chatter around the table had become easier. She hadn't realised they were all being careful until they weren't.

'So, where do you recommend I go to finish up my Christmas shopping?' Fiona's question made her husband chuckle. 'Why're you laughing?'

'We paid an arm and a leg to bring a third suitcase full of gifts with us. What more do you need to buy?'

'Those were baby clothes.'

'Oh yeah, of course, because they don't sell them here.' He smacked the side of his head. 'The Brits don't have babies.'

Her mother ignored him and turned back to Ashley. 'I know you're snowed under with work so just steer us in the right direction.'

'Truro's your best bet. It's a cute market town and there

are regular buses you can catch from Polgarth. Did you have a chance to check out all the festival stalls today for gifts or were you baby worshipping?' Fiona's flushed face was a giveaway. 'Enough said. You'll have another chance next weekend if that's not too late.'

'You're enjoying all this, aren't you?'

Her mother's wistfulness was palpable. The reality had sunk in that Ashley wouldn't be rushing to live back in Tennessee anytime soon.

'Yeah, I absolutely love it, and I've got heaps of ideas to expand both businesses.' They'd been extremely close until she married with few of the battles that marred so many teenage girls' relationships with their mothers. Bunny's controlling behaviour put a wedge between them and she ached to put that right. 'You're here for a good while yet, so we've plenty of time for a proper chat.'

'Have *you* finished your Christmas shopping, Crispin?' Her mother's casual question sent a flash of panic skittering across his face. 'Got you there, haven't I?'

A deep red flush mottled his neck and everyone burst out laughing. Ashley felt a niggle of guilt because Christmas shopping hadn't made her to-do list either, but she kept that to herself. They still had two full weeks left before Christmas Day. Plenty of time.

Chapter Twenty-Two

Crispin stared at the steaming mug of tea Nessa put in front of him and grimaced. 'What am I going to do?' The conversation with Ashley's mother about Christmas shopping had haunted him since the weekend, and with only ten days left now until the big day he couldn't bury it under a rock any longer.

'Start by making a list.'

He'd never bought enough Christmas presents to need a list. Rhonda was happy with the standard Marks & Spencer gift card he gave her every year – at least he assumed she was.

'You're really at a loss, aren't you?' A tiny smirk tweaked the corners of her mouth.

'Does Ward do his own or do you do it for him?'

'Do my own what?' Ward strolled in, tugged out a chair and joined them.

'Christmas shopping.' Nessa beamed at her husband. 'Crispin probably isn't going to believe this but you're awesome at gift buying. You need to take him in hand.'

'Sure. I'm happy to help. How many are we lookin' at? You'll be here on Christmas Day, so everyone I guess?'

The more names he rattled off, the lower Crispin's spirits sank.

'You got anythin' big goin' on today? If you don't, we could sneak off for a few hours.'

He couldn't conjure up a viable excuse.

'I'll make it as painless as possible. Tris's down for his

nap good, so he's all yours Nessa. If anyone needs us, we'll be back by tea time.'

Crispin must have failed to hide his dismay because Ward's rumbling laugh filled the kitchen.

'Don't panic. It shouldn't take that long, but the traffic is bound to be shitty. The sooner we get goin' the better.'

Half an hour later, he and Ward were stuck in a seemingly endless crawl of cars.

'You got any ideas for specific people?'

'Uh, not really.' While they inched along, Crispin was treated to an interrogation worthy of MI5. What people liked. Their hobbies. Anything they'd mentioned having an interest in. By the time they snagged a space in one of the car parks, Crispin felt wrung out but mildly triumphant. 'Nessa was right about you.'

'It's not hard if you pay attention.' Ward's smile turned mischievous. 'Scores points with women too, which is never a bad thing. C'mon, it's time to put the battle plan into action.'

They shopped in the way of determined, focused men, eating a snatched pasty lunch out of paper bags while they made their way from one end of the town to the other.

'You've done good. There's only Ashley left on your list.' Ward looked satisfied. 'If you're thinkin' on the lines of lingerie, you're on your own. My sister and all that. Too weird. Take an hour by yourself to see to hers. I've a few things to pick up myself so I'll meet you back at the car park.'

Thirty minutes later when he still hadn't found anything, panic was setting in and he dived into one of the narrow side streets by the ancient cathedral to escape the crowds.

Crispin pushed open the door of the first small shop he came to.

'Careful, my 'andsome.' A smiling, grey-haired woman hurried over to him. Her bright red Christmas jumper was stretched over her ample curves so the squat stretched-out reindeer looked as if it'd lost its footing on a sheet of ice.

'Sorry.' He suddenly noticed the display of colourful pottery standing perilously close to his right elbow.

'Do you want some help finding a Christmas present?'

Crispin assumed he wasn't the only clueless male she'd had to deal with today. He took a proper look around and realised he was surrounded by the famous striped china known as Cornishware. Ashley had told him only the other day that she'd fallen in love with this design. She'd never seen it before Lowena moved her own extensive set into the Tregereth kitchen.

'Please. My ... girlfriend likes this china. I'm not sure what to get though?'

'Do you want the original blue or the newer red or yellow.'

'Blue.' His emphasis made the woman smile. Lowena's china was blue so he wasn't going to take a risk by deviating.

'What does she have already?'

'Nothing.' Crispin wasn't sure if that made it easier or harder.

'How about a teapot and cups or mugs to start her off? You can't go wrong with that.'

'I could. She's not a tea drinker.' Something struck him. 'She's started to do some baking, so maybe a few plates?'

'I've got just the thing, love.' She beckoned him over to the window. 'How about one of these pretty cake stands? They'd gone out of fashion 'til that baking show made them popular again. We sell out of them all the time, but you're lucky because I had a new delivery yesterday.'

'Perfect. I'll take that, some plates as well, and maybe mugs? She drinks coffee but they'd do for either, wouldn't they?'

'They certainly would. How many of each do you want? Half a dozen maybe?'

'Sounds good.' Crispin pulled out his wallet. 'I don't suppose you wrap things?'

'We certainly do.' Her grey eyes twinkled. 'You're a good man to take all this trouble. We can't resist a man who does that.'

Exactly what he hoped.

Ashley peered around the crowds of people gathered outside the floodlit church for the village carol singing but couldn't see anyone from Pear Tree Farm.

'Daddy, Daddy! Come here.' Rhys wriggled out of his mother's grasp and jumped up and down waving madly, and she spotted Crispin weaving his way towards them. The broad smile lighting him up was a million miles away from the dour man she'd first met. She knew it probably wasn't vain to claim part of that was down to her, but the precious little boy next to her played a huge part too. Whatever Samira's motive, Ashley would always be grateful to the woman for giving Crispin the chance to know his son.

'Well, who's this? Are you one of Father Christmas's

139

elves?' He tugged on the boy's red felt hat with its dangling silver bell. Ashley had bought it for him last week at the festival and he'd refused to take it off, even to sleep.

'Silly Daddy.'

Crispin swung his smile her way. 'I've been Christmas shopping today.'

'You? Voluntarily?'

'Sort of.' He shuffled his feet. 'Nessa set Ward on me.'

'That figures. My brother's weird that way. Gives awesome gifts though.' Ashley snuggled up to him. 'You'll raise everyone's expectations if the word gets around he's been mentoring you.'

'Consider the challenge met.' He slipped his arm around her waist and whispered in her ear. 'Any chance you might visit "Mr Blue Sky" after this?'

'I could be talked into it.' Ashley glanced around. 'Did you come on your own? Where's everyone else?'

'Tristan has a bit of a sniffle so Nessa didn't want to bring him out in the cold. Ward stayed with them and your parents—'

'Stayed because little Tris needs four adults fussing over him.' She sighed. 'I can't blame them for making the most of it. It's gonna be so hard when they've got to leave. All the decisions we make have ripples, don't they?'

'You're not regretting—'

'Daddy, I can't see. Mummy says I'm too heavy to lift up.' Rhys tugged on Crispin's leg, and with a fleeting shrug at her he hoisted the boy on his shoulders.

Although she felt a brief sliver of annoyance at being interrupted in the middle of an important conversation, Ashley made sure to smile because the last thing they needed was Samira getting the wrong idea. She'd never resent him paying attention to his son.

The small brass band, consisting of about half a dozen villagers who relied on volume rather than musical ability, struck up 'Hark the Herald Angels Sing'. Thankfully Crispin's strong melodious voice covered up the worst of the off-key music.

'Are you staying for the mulled wine and mince pies?' Lowena sidled around to join her. 'I hear it's all homemade.'

'The question is, were they made by someone who knows what they're doin'?' She stifled a giggle. The previous evening, the two of them spent hours baking mince pies and mixing alcoholic and non-alcoholic versions of mulled wine before delivering them to the church hall this morning. 'If you don't mind, I might give it a miss.'

'You've got a better offer?'

The cold night air had no effect on her flaming cheeks.

'Good. The two of you need more time together.' Lowena angled a disapproving look in Samira's direction. Her friend had no qualms about voicing her opinion that Rhys's mother hadn't given up on her quest to win Crispin back. 'I'll take care of our guests.'

'Thanks.'

The band leader announced that 'Away in a Manger' would be the last carol, and tears welled up in her eyes as the poignant music started. Crispin set Rhys back down by his mother and slipped an arm around Ashley's shoulder.

'Okay?'

'I will be.' She buried her face in his thick black coat and managed to pull herself together as the familiar song ended.

'Are you coming with us for mince pies?' Samira planted herself in front of them.

'No, but Lowena's goin' and she offered to take care of you both. She'll give you a lift back to Tregereth.'

'We've got plans.'

Crispin spoke up, and she noticed his ex's brief flicker of distaste before it was covered with a faint smile. Ashley watched him bend down to hug Rhys but he stepped away when Samira tried to touch his arm.

They strolled back through the village, chatting to a few people they knew along the way and checked out the variety of Christmas decorations they spotted in the various houses. It stirred up a clash between his preference for the coloured lights of his childhood and her own for simple white ones. His strong, comforting hand clasped hers and his veiled eyes gleamed in the dark every time he glanced her way.

As they walked into the farm a shiver ran through her. 'Don't you find it a bit eerie here in the winter? Apart from the farmhouse and Polly and Jack, there's no one around.'

'Doesn't bother me. I like the peace and quiet.' He angled her a questioning look. 'I could say the same for you at Tregereth. Apart from the few festival weekend guests you're having, and Samira and Rhys, it's only been you and Lowena rattling around that big place since October. Kit will be gone back to college in another couple of weeks.'

'I suppose you're right.' It struck her for the first time that she couldn't see herself living and working there alone if Lowena ever left. Ashley was afraid that if she admitted that it might sound like an invitation of some sort. 'C'mon, I'm getting cold.' Two bear-like arms wrapped around her and Crispin nuzzled her face with his warm nose. 'Okay, that's enough Bigfoot.'

'I'll soon warm you up.'

'Promises. Promises.'

They hurried up the path to "Mr Blue Sky" and he fumbled with the key before managing to wrench the door open. The short path to the bedroom was soon strewn with their clothes, and Ashley yanked him down to her.

'God, it's been too long,' she complained. 'We've gotta do better than this.'

'I'm in agreement there.'

Much, much later he offered to move, but she loved the heavy weight of him pinning her to the bed and begged him to stay wrapped around her.

'You want to talk about us first or Samira?' Crispin asked.

'Aren't they kind of the same thing?' She started to expand on her belief that his ex-girlfriend hadn't given up on the idea of them reconnecting.

'But I made things clear to her. You know that.'

'Yeah, but I'm not the only one who doesn't believe she got the message.'

'The way I saw it, Samira and I were the typical two ships in a storm finding a harbour with each other. Once the storm passed that was it … at least it was for me. I never once told her I loved her, not even …' His raspy voice trailed away. 'Well, you know.'

'Yeah, I know.' People said things in the throes of passion that didn't stand up in the light of day.

'I don't know what else I can do or say to convince her … or maybe I do.' Crispin's sexy smile made her tingle all over. 'I'm a one-woman man these days and I'm looking at her. Do you think she feels the same way and is okay with everyone knowing that?'

Ashley's heart raced. 'What do you mean exactly?'

'Exactly? Do you think an engagement ring would work?'

When she didn't immediately respond, Crispin's face fell.

'You're not a fan of the idea? I was stupid to think you might be.' He rolled off her and sat cross-legged with his hands wrapped around his scarred knees. Only the other night he'd told her the story behind those lasting mementoes of another bad day in Afghanistan.

'Don't jump to conclusions. I wasn't sure if you meant it for real or whether you're talkin' a fake thing to throw Samira off the scent?'

'I know it wasn't the most romantic proposal and—'

'Move in with me.' Her out-of-the-blue suggestion made his jaw drop. 'It'd give us a chance to get to know each other better, and maybe in a while I might not—'

'Be so appalled at the idea of marrying me?' The cheerful lilt to his voice encouraged her to be honest.

'I wasn't appalled. Far from it. I'm flattered, but it's too soon. For both of us.' His searching look unnerved her. 'It should kick Samira's plans for you to the kerb too so it's a win all around.'

'Okay. You've got a deal.' Crispin tilted another smile her way. 'Unromantic maybe, but we aren't great on that, are we?'

'Oh, I don't know about that. Depends how you define the word.' She toyed with the swirls of silky dark hair covering his broad chest until he got the hint and swooped her back down on the bed.

She pushed the idea that she was being reckless with a man again to the back of her mind.

Chapter Twenty-Three

'If Ash and Lowena suggest doin' this again next year, remind me to gag them.' Ward eased down on the nearest chair. 'Don't know about you, mate, but I'm knackered.'

'I'm pretty beat too.' Crispin admitted. They'd spent all morning getting all of the festival gear packed away and fresh gravel laid on the paths that'd borne the brunt of thousands of pounding feet over the last few weeks. Of course, part of his exhaustion could be laid at Ashley's door because she'd sneaked into his caravan each of the last four nights, but he wasn't complaining about that.

'But it was so worth it,' Nessa protested. 'Look how much money we made and we got loads more bookings for my garden-to-table classes and for the camp site.' Her cheeks turned bright pink. 'I've got to admit though that I did hardly any of the work, but another time I promise I'll be more involved.'

He suppressed a smile when Ward hurried to backtrack and assure his wife that she'd been landed with full time parenting duties while he'd been busy so she had nothing to apologise for.

'I'd better get cleaned up for lunch.' Crispin tugged his coat off the back of the chair and slipped it on again.

'You don't need to sound as though you're going to your execution. It'll be fun.'

Nessa had issued a three-line whip for Sunday lunch at the pub to wrap up their exertions and everyone had orders to be at The Chough on the dot of noon to fit around Tristan's nap times. Polly and Jack were missing out because they were still in Birmingham. Ashley's ploy had worked. The couple had travelled up together and were due back by mid-week in time for Christmas.

'I'm sure Ash will hold your hand and protect you from Mom's inquisition.' Ward teased. 'You don't have to worry. We've all given you a decent reference.'

'I appreciate it.' They'd be embarrassed if he laboured the point about how much he owed them.

'Just don't fall asleep this time and be late.'

Behind Nessa's back he laughingly gave Ward the middle finger before striding off.

'Did I get my instructions wrong?' Crispin stared at Ashley perched on the steps of "Mr Blue Sky" when he reached the caravan. 'I thought we were meeting outside the pub?'

'We were.' She unravelled herself and bounced over to wrap her arms around his neck. 'I couldn't wait that long.'

A rush of heat spread through his body as she moulded herself against him and the intoxicating scent of warm spices surrounded him. 'You smell wonderful. New perfume?'

'Oh yeah, it's Eau de Mince Pies.' Her laughter aroused him. 'Lowena insisted we needed more for all the visitors she swears we'll have over the holidays. Apparently if you don't offer everyone who stops by a glass of sherry and a mince pie you'll be ostracised.'

'Can't have that.' Her cold cheek pressed against his. 'Let's go in before we freeze.' The rain had been replaced by unusually frigid temperatures. 'I need to shower.'

'Want an audience?'

'You're wicked.'

'Yeah, that's me.'

Crispin glanced at his watch. 'I don't want to piss off your parents by being late for lunch.' He checked out her sleek black top, wide-legged red trousers and black ankle boots. 'It won't help my case if you look ravished when we arrive.'

'In that case, I guess we'll save the ravishing for later.'

'That's a date.' He steered her towards the sofa. 'Stay out here.'

'Vain man. Anyone would think I can't stand within two feet of you and not want to jump your bones,' Ashley scoffed.

Crispin hummed 'Myfanway', an old Welsh song about a cruel woman, under his breath as he hurried away. He dressed in the same black trousers, this time with a dark navy jumper, then rubbed a hand over his rough chin. Yesterday's shave wasn't going to hack it. After wielding the razor once more he strolled back out to join Ashley.

'How's that?' This reminded him of going on parade and being inspected by the Regimental Colonel.

'You'll do.' Ashley's smile overrode her laconic reply. 'We'd better go.'

'We're early.'

'If we don't leave now, you're the one who'll arrive looking ravished.'

He gamely suppressed a smirk and shrugged on his black wool coat.

'You forgot something.' Ashley unhitched his Cornish tartan scarf from the hook by the door and knotted it around his neck. 'Is this a disloyal thing for a Welshman to wear?'

'Don't worry about it.' As long as she kept smiling and worshipping him with her eyes that way, he'd happily dress head to toe in the tartan and wouldn't give a damn.

'So, what did you think of your first English Sunday lunch, Mom?' Ashley smiled at her mother's empty plate. 'I'm guessing you didn't like it?' Now over the worst of their jet-lag, her parents were throwing themselves whole-heartedly into every local tradition, Christmas or otherwise. She could already picture Fiona throwing an English themed party next December for her less well-travelled friends.

'Lowena's promised me a lesson on making Yorkshire puddings one day this week.' Her mother quickly switched her attention over to Crispin. 'Tell me more about your family back in Wales.'

'There's only my older sister, Rhonda. Our parents died a long time ago.'

'Is she coming here for Christmas?'

'Uh … no.'

When Ashley had asked him the same thing the other day, he'd brushed it off by saying he'd been away for so many holiday seasons over the years that they'd fallen out of the habit. That was something she hoped to change.

'My son tells me you're a singer.' Her father leaned across. 'I'm lookin' forward to hearing you on Christmas Eve.'

'What're you talkin' about, Dad?'

'The Wheal Boys are doing an evening of old Cornish carols and your clever brother's written a new song for them. They've talked this guy here into joining them.'

'Really? It's the first I've heard about it.' She gave Crispin an arched look. 'Were you goin' to tell me at some point or just surprise me?'

'I didn't mean to *not* tell you.' He squirmed in the chair. 'Ward steered me into a corner the other day and I agreed to run through a couple of songs with him yesterday to put a stop to the daft idea. Somehow, next thing I find I'm agreeing to sing two numbers with him and the rest of the group. I must need my head tested,' Crispin muttered.

'You'll be awesome.' Ashley popped a kiss on his cheek. A voice like Crispin's deserved a wider audience than the rows of cabbages and carrots in the garden.

'I'll get you signed up to a record label if you aren't careful. I've still got plenty of contacts in the music business.'

'Dad's joking.' Ashley hoped he'd get the hint to back off. 'Have you finished your Christmas shopping, Mom?' Her mother didn't need any urging to chatter about the great time they'd had in Truro. She wasn't the only one struggling not to laugh when Fiona lowered her voice to describe everything she'd bought for Tristan as if it would spoil the surprise for the not quite three-month-old dozing on Nessa's shoulder.

'Is *your* shopping all done?' Crispin turned the question right back at her.

'Mine? Not really.' *Not at all would be more truthful.*

'Do you need any help?' His deep blue eyes sparkled with mischief.

'I'll be fine, thank you. I'm dedicating tomorrow to the task.' With less than a week until Christmas, she'd be joining all the other frantic shoppers in the last-minute battle. She turned back to her parents. 'Do you have any other plans apart from cooking lessons?'

'Your daddy's going with Ward and Rhys to the ice rink at the Eden Project tomorrow.' Fiona beamed at Crispin. 'You've got a lovely boy there.'

'I can't take any of the credit. You know that.'

Crispin's inability to be anything other than honest made him a keeper as far as she was concerned.

'Where are Rhys and Samira today? I thought they'd be here.'

'Nessa invited them but they've made some friends in the village and they're getting together today to take the kids to one of those soft play area places.'

'Oh, Rhys will love that. What are your plans when he goes off with his mom again? I guess you'll visit him when you can and bring him back here for holidays?'

'Mom, please. Let's not discuss this now.'

'It's all right. I don't mind.' Crispin covered her hand with his own. 'Those are details I need to sort out with Samira. With Ashley's help.'

That brought satisfied smiles to her parents' faces.

'Who's for dessert?' Ward pointed to the chalkboard on the wall. 'The sticky toffee pudding is out of this world.'

'I'm stuffed.' Fiona patted her stomach. 'I see someone's awake so I'm ready to be granny again.' She held out her hands to Nessa. 'Hand that dear boy over. We're gonna walk around and look at the pretty Christmas things, aren't we, my sweet?'

'I need to finish wrapping my presents so I'll be on my way.' Lowena gathered up her coat and handbag. 'Thank you for lunch.'

Ashley didn't challenge her but knew an excuse when she heard one. Weeks ago, her friend had boasted before they had their Christmas festival weekends that her own holiday preparations were complete. Her stomach clenched when she watched her father slide into the vacant chair by Crispin. They didn't need any more questions about their plans for the future today. 'Dessert, Dad?'

'Good Lord girl, if I eat another thing they'll roll me onto the plane home.' Todd laughed. 'Whoever said English food was lousy didn't know what they were talkin' about.'

'Is no one joinin' me?' Ward's disappointment increased when even Nessa begged off. 'You're all lightweights.'

'Somethin' you won't be after another bowl of sticky toffee pudding!' Teasing her brother was ingrained in her DNA. 'You can fetch me a coffee if you don't mind.'

'Me too. I'll give you a hand.' Nessa sprang up as well, leaving the three of them alone.

The background music turned from regular carols to the well-known tones of 'Merry Christmas Everybody'. She'd come to the grim conclusion that it was mathematically impossible to escape the dreadful song that played non-stop in England from November onwards. Ashley had never heard of Slade before moving here, but apparently the group was popular back in the eighties – something she'd never understand if she lived to be a hundred.

'While Fiona's out of the way …' Her father gave a surreptitious glance around.

'You want to know whether I'm going to live in a caravan and do odd-jobs around Pear Tree Farm long term, sir?' Crispin's blunt interruption made her cringe. 'The answer is I don't know.'

'I'm sure he wasn't going to ask that – were you, Daddy?'

She could have died of embarrassment when her father's face turned puce.

'It's all right, he's just being a good father. He sees red flags because of the troubles I've had and what he's seen of my life now.'

Crispin's measured response took the edge off her anger while it simultaneously broke her heart. If she said he was trustworthy, loyal and completely honest, that made Crispin sound like a much-loved pet, but to her mind those qualities topped having a prestigious job and a million dollars in the bank. It was time she broke her silence and told her parents the full extent of what had gone on in her marriage.

'There are things I need to share with you and Mom.' Ashley went for it. 'I'd like the four of us to get together tomorrow.' She managed to smile. 'Let's make it after Tris is in bed so you don't miss out on baby-worshipping time. How about we meet at "Mr Blue Sky?"' Her father's puzzlement made her laugh. 'That's Crispin's caravan. Nessa named them all after her favourite summer songs.' She caught sight of her mother and Tristan heading their way. 'Don't you wish we had pubs like this back home?' Her dad looked confused until he caught sight of them too.

'Oh yeah. I sure do, honey.'

The shine had gone off the day and Ashley already dreaded telling her parents things they wouldn't want to hear.

Chapter Twenty-Four

Crispin was locking up the barn when he spotted Ward's truck pull up in front of the farmhouse and his friend jump out. The other doors opened and Todd, Samira and Rhys all clambered out too.

In the army he'd had no problem with being decisive, but since then the days, weeks and months had slipped away almost unnoticed. and he hadn't given much thought to making any plans for the future until Ashley came into his life. When he second-guessed her father's question yesterday, it made him realise he needed a long overdue conversation with Ward. Todd Spencer deserved a proper answer tonight.

'Come and join us, Crispin!' Nessa was standing in the farmhouse door and yelled over to him. 'I'll put the kettle on and we can hear all about the skating expedition.'

'Cheers.' Crispin toed off his muddy boots and set them by the step.

'Daddy, carry me. I'm tired.' Rhys ran over and held up his arms. Across the little boy's shoulder, he caught the glimmer of satisfaction in Samira's eyes.

'Let's get in the kitchen.' Nessa encouraged everyone in out of the cold. 'How about some Christmas cake? Don't worry, I didn't make it. I bought it at the festival.' She cut small slices of fruitcake and offered them around the table once everyone was sitting down.

'Not for me, thanks.' Ward's father lumbered to his feet. 'I don't know about anyone else but I need a lie down. I'm gonna blame jet-lag, not the fact I shouldn't have tried to keep up with the boy.' He rubbed his backside. 'I'll feel those falls on the ice tomorrow. Where's Fiona?'

'She's up at Tregereth with Lowena. Some kind of baking's goin' on, I think.'

'Oh Lord, not more food.' He patted his stomach. 'Even more reason to take a nap.'

'Ward, can we have a quick word?' Crispin didn't like to ask his friend if they could talk in private and guessed his awkwardness was obvious when Nessa suggested to Samira that they moved into the living room.

'Can Daddy come too?' Rhys piped up.

'I need your daddy for a while, but I promise we won't be long.' Ward's effort to placate the boy didn't work and he looked close to tears, making Crispin feel even worse.

'Rudolph the Red-nosed Reindeer is just starting on the TV, and if you're a good boy you can choose one of the chocolate Christmas decorations hanging on the tree.' Nessa worked her usual magic and Rhys raced off without a backward glance.

'You wanna get some fresh air?'

'Sure.' Crispin dragged his coat back on and they walked outside. They wandered up to the walled garden and chatted about improvements to make before they opened again at Easter, then checked on the Brussels sprouts to make sure there'd be enough for lunch on Christmas Day.

'I'm not goin' to play the interfering older brother card, so put that out of your head.'

He might have guessed yesterday's conversation would have found its way back. 'I know but I still need to get my act together.' Embarrassment burned his cheeks. 'You know I love Ashley.'

'Well, yeah. I'd have to be dumb not to see that. I'm guessin' you've told her?'

He shook his head. 'Not in so many words. It's early days, I know, but … maybe I've experienced more of how unpredictable life is so I don't want to drag my feet too long.' He didn't plan to mention Ashley's offer for him to move in with her yet.

'It's okay, I get it. Nessa and I had some things to work through when we met too. I guess what I'm sayin' is we all have obstacles. They're different ones, that's all.' Ward shoved his hands in his pockets. 'We've talked a lot recently about getting things on a more solid footing in the new year. Both businesses being so successful has brought its own problems, and you know the workload at both places is increasing. Jack is interested in buying some of the land to the east of the top field that's sitting idle. They want to build a little bungalow. Nessa's agreeable so that'll free up some assets for us to expand.' He gave Crispin a long look. 'Lowena dropped a bit of a surprise on us this morning.'

'Oh God, I hope she's not leaving? Ashley will have a fit!'

'Don't panic.' Ward chuckled. 'She's keeping her job but wants to move out of Tregereth and buy her own place. There's a cottage in Polgarth near the church she's got her eye on. It's not huge but she'll have enough space for Kit too. It'll save him paying rent in at St Austell when he's at college.'

'How's he getting on with his course? I haven't had a chance to ask.'

'Loves it.' Ward smiled. 'It's thanks to you and my darling wife that he discovered a passion for digging in the dirt. Once he gets his degree, it should give him his pick of jobs anywhere he fancies.' His expression turned more serious. 'For a minute, this is me floating an idea so don't think anything's written in stone. Listen to what we've come up with and talk it over with Ash.'

Crispin's heart pounded.

This must be what it was like to do a few rounds with Muhammad Ali, Ashley thought. She made it back to the car park in one piece after fighting through the throngs of people, all determined to finish their Christmas shopping. To describe her festive spirit as flagging was the understatement of the decade.

After wandering around for a few minutes on the wrong floor, she tracked down her car. Her very own car. She'd recently treated herself to a brand-new bright turquoise Volkswagen Polo after becoming tired of borrowing vehicles every time she wanted to go somewhere. It felt like another statement that she intended to stay. A text popped in from Crispin while she was loading her shopping bags in the boot.

Come early. We need to talk x

What did he need to say that couldn't be spelled out in front of her parents? She replied then set her phone aside to join the lengthening queue of cars battling to get out of Truro.

Lowena had whisked Samira and Rhys off to Mousehole to see the famous Christmas lights so the house felt large, gloomy and empty when she opened the front door. It struck like a thunderbolt that it would soon be like this all the time. This morning her friend shocked her when she sprang the news that she was buying a house in the village.

When Lowena expressed concern about leaving Ashley there alone, it'd felt wrong not to speak up and tell Lowena she'd asked Crispin to move in, but now she was relieved she'd held her tongue. Perhaps he'd changed his mind? She hauled her shopping up to the bedroom and hid the bags out of sight in the back of the wardrobe then headed straight down to the farm.

Ashley waved at Nessa who was standing at the kitchen window and parked in the reserved space outside "Mr Blue Sky". Her spirits lifted when Crispin popped his head out of the door and broke into a wide smile at the sight of her. He wouldn't be capable of hiding his feelings this well if he intended on giving her bad news.

'Have you eaten?'

'No.' Ashley ran up the steps and flung her arms around his neck. 'Kiss me first, then you can feed me.'

'I don't mind doing that.'

They indulged themselves for a few wonderful moments before he pulled away.

'I've got big news … well, not exactly news … more of a possibility. I'm not sure what you'll think of it and—'

'Stop there.' She touched a finger to his lips. 'Let's go inside. It's cold.' She followed him in. 'Something smells good. Let me guess. Chicken soup?' His brow furrowed but she couldn't hold onto her straight face any longer. The smell of pasties cooking was unmistakeable, even to a native Tennessean.

'They've just come out of the oven and need to cool off a bit.'

'Let's sit down.' She plopped down on the narrow sofa and patted the space next to her. 'Out with it.'

'I needed to sort some things before your parents arrive for the chat you've got planned with them, so I had a word with Ward earlier.' Crispin clamped his hands on his thighs and looked nervous.

By the time he ran out of breath a few minutes later, Ashley was stunned.

'What do you think?'

It was a struggle to keep her voice neutral. 'So, what you're basically sayin' is Ward's offering you a partnership in Tregereth as a sort of dowry? I suppose it's so my family won't have to fret about whether I'm coping alone ...'

'No!' Crispin recoiled. 'How can you think that way? It's a business proposition, plain and simple. I thought you'd be pleased. For me. For us.'

Guilt washed over her.

'You know I'm doing most of the maintenance work at Tregereth anyway so that wouldn't change, but right now I've only got time to do the basics in the garden. It's got so much potential that I'd enjoy exploring if Ward takes on someone else to do my jobs at Pear Tree Farm.'

'If you weren't so determined to impress my parents, would you have pushed for this?'

'I don't know.' His honesty made her anger seep away. 'What I'm trying to get across is that Ward was all set to approach me anyway. He and Nessa have been talking this over for months, before we ever got together, and they're going to make a similar offer to Lowena.' A smile twitched his lips. 'I swear mine isn't dependent on me marrying you and hers won't be either.'

'Marrying me?'

'In case you're worried, I didn't tell him you'd asked me to move in with you.' Wariness took over his face. 'I hadn't spelled it out yet because I'm not good at that sort of thing … but I love you more than anything, and I know you're perfectly capable of taking care of yourself and don't "need me". I hoped you'd see this as helping us to build a solid life together … have I screwed up as usual?'

'No, you haven't. I overreacted.'

'So, you're happy for me to accept Ward's offer?'

'Yeah, I definitely am.'

'It'll be a challenge but I'm ready for that.' His steady gaze made the heat rise in her face. They both knew this wasn't simply about stepping up as far as work was concerned but a whole lot more. 'We don't *need* a piece of paper or rings … but if one day you *want* them, you'll have to be the one to say so.'

She battled Bunny's lingering effect on her confidence on a daily basis, but Crispin was placing her in the driver's seat. 'That sounds perfect and in case *you* weren't certain, I love you too. I know you've still got to work through things with Samira goin' forward, but I'm with you a hundred per cent on being the best dad you can be to Rhys. Now, if I have to smell those pasties any longer and not get my hands on one, I'm goin' to lose it.'

'We can't have that.'

By the time her father knocked on the door, they'd eaten, laughed and sneaked more than a few kisses. Ashley couldn't control the huge grin on her face when she let them in. 'Come in, we've got some awesome news.' Everything bubbled out of her and her parents couldn't have been more pleased about Crispin's partnership offer, but their smiles became more guarded when she announced they were planning to move in together.

'I'm not tryin' to interfere honey, but have you both thought this through good?' Her father's forehead creased in a worried frown. 'No offence, Crispin but—'

'None taken.'

Time to take the bull by the horns, she thought. 'You need to hear a few home truths about my marriage so you'll know where I'm comin' from. I wanted to protect you before from the details, but it's important you understand why I'm so sure now that what Crispin and I share is something special and precious.' Ashley took a couple of deep breaths then held nothing back. By the time she finished everyone had tears in their eyes.

'Oh, my poor love.' Fiona's voice caught in a sob. 'I'm sorry that Bunny fooled me as long as he did. You should've been able to rely on our support ... I'll always regret that you couldn't.'

'Don't beat yourself up, Mom. Everything worked out for the best and I couldn't be happier now.'

'That's all we need to know.' Her father grasped Ashley's hand and nodded towards Crispin. 'The two of you deserve all the happiness in the world. Anythin' we can do to help, you just tell us.'

'Thanks for trusting me.' Crispin's attempt to control his emotions tugged at her heart. 'It means a lot.'

It struck her that Christmas miracles came early in Cornwall.

Chapter Twenty-Five

Crispin hauled the last of his bags outside and dumped them by the steps. He shoved his hands deep in his pockets and wash of emotions flooded through him as he gazed around the site, bathed this morning in pale winter sunshine.

An interesting evening was one way of describing how the previous night had turned out to be. For the first time, Fiona and Todd realised what their daughter had endured and her true strength. After that it made no sense to delay, so here he was all packed and ready to leave.

He heard a car approaching, and next thing Ashley parked in front of "Mr Blue Sky" and jumped right out.

'Ready to load up? I hope you haven't changed your mind?'

He must have been frowning. 'Not unless you've changed yours about sharing that king-sized bed you keep boasting about?' Crispin wrapped his hands around her waist and rested his thumbs on the wide black leather belt circling her dark red knitted dress. 'Are you sure Lowena's okay with me coming? We didn't give her much warning.'

'She thinks it's awesome. Her offer on that cottage has been accepted and it's empty so the seller is letting her rent it while the paperwork goes through. Ward told me what a rigmarole y'all have for house sales. Apparently it usually takes months. She'll stay at Tregereth through the holidays then move straight out. Kit will help her to get settled before his course starts again in the New Year.' Her smile widened even further. 'What did my dear brother and Nessa have to say when you broke the news?'

Crispin felt his face redden. 'Ward made a slightly raunchy comment and Nessa smacked him. She almost broke my ribs hugging me and said it was the best news she'd heard in forever.'

'Par for the course then.' She gave him a hard stare. 'In case you were wondering, I told Samira our good news at breakfast.'

'You read my mind.'

'It's not that hard. You might be good at hiding your feelings from other people but you're crap at it around me.' A smug edge crept into her honeyed drawl. 'Samira didn't have much to say.'

'Maybe I should—'

'Postpone? Nope.' The gold flecks in her eyes gleamed. 'This is the ideal time. It'll kick any lingering hope she's got of hooking up with you again to the kerb.' Ashley's smile faded. 'I shouldn't have said that. It was mean.'

'It's okay.' Crispin caressed her face, smoothing his fingers over the now familiar contours that he could've drawn blindfolded. 'We only do honesty, remember? Now, are we going to load up your car and get on our way?'

'Is this all you've got?' She pointed to the backpack, two black bin bags and three small cardboard boxes.

He guessed there weren't many men heading for forty who owned so little. 'Yep, and some of that's kitchen gear and towels and stuff, so I won't take up much of your wardrobe space. I'll lock up and drop the key in to Nessa on our way out.'

'I see lights on at Polly and Jack's. Did you know they were back?'

'No, they must've got in late last night.' Crispin frowned. 'It's funny they didn't knock on my door to say hello.'

'Let's go find out how they're doin'.' Ashley linked her arm through his. 'Come on.'

Jack opened the door at Crispin's first knock and managed a tired attempt at a smile. 'Thought it would be you. Come in. Polly's just got up.'

'I don't have my face on and my hair's a mess. Consider yourselves warned.' Polly padded out from the bedroom in the middle of cinching the belt on her pink fluffy dressing-gown. 'Nessa told me your bit of news. You sneaky pair.' She patted her hair which right now resembled a fading purple bird's nest. 'It's a good thing my regular appointment is in three days is all I know.'

'Will you be turning it red and green for Christmas?' Crispin's question made her face crumple.

'I'm not sure I'll be in the mood, lovey ... we lost my sister last week.'

'Oh Polly, I'm sorry.'

'Me too.' His old friend's bright blue eyes filled with tears.

'But we had time to talk first, didn't we love?' Jack slipped an arm around his wife's shoulders. 'It made all the difference in the world.'

'It certainly did and I've you to thank for that.' Polly nodded at Ashley.

'Me?'

'You told me I'd regret it if I left it too late, and now I can't imagine what it would've been like to hear the news about Meg and realise I wouldn't have the chance to put things right with her.' The ghost of a smile brightened her sad expression. 'We've spoken to Nessa already and booked all of the caravans for the last weekend before Easter so a whole group of our family can come down to visit.'

'That'll be awesome. I can't wait to meet them all.'

Polly peered out over Crispin's shoulder. 'Got your bags packed, I see. We're going to miss you.'

He swallowed hard and managed to nod, dropping his head so they couldn't see the tears blurring his eyes.

'You look after our boy now.' Polly wagged a finger at Ashley and then gave Crispin a playful jab in the ribs. 'And you take care of her. If you both do that, you'll be all right. Now off you go and we'll see you over Christmas.'

They said their goodbyes, and five minutes later he fought down another rush of emotion as they drove out of Pear Tree Farm together. Ashley left him alone and didn't say another word until she parked outside the grand front door of Tregereth House. It was decorated for Christmas with a fresh holly wreath sporting a red shiny bow, and he noticed similar ones hanging in all of the windows.

'Welcome home.'

If he had any lingering reservations, they disappeared when he heard those words.

'I wanted to let you know our plans have changed.' Samira cornered Ashley by the sink where she was on dishwashing duty.

Everyone had gravitated to the kitchen which was warm and fragrant with spices and the hum of carols from the radio. They'd soon be buried under a mountain of mince pies because Lowena was baking again, and this time she'd roped in Kit and his girlfriend Lucy so they had a production line going on. Lucy's parents were in Australia visiting their son and his family for the holidays so the young woman was staying with them here too. Crispin was sitting at one end of the table with his excited son curled up on his lap. From the snippets of conversation she'd picked up, they were discussing what Father Christmas might bring them both.

'We're leaving on Boxing Day.'

'That soon?' Was she a bad person to feel a tiny sliver of relief? she wondered.

'I think it's best, don't you?' A faint hint of admiration curved Samira's full mouth. 'You've made your point. I know where I stand now.'

'I totally meant it when I said I'll never put any obstacle in the way of Crispin being a good father to Rhys.' That needed to be perfectly clear. She never wanted him to accuse her of being less than encouraging on that score. 'Have you told them yet?' She nodded towards the table.

'No. I don't want to spoil Christmas. It'll be time enough once we're through with Christmas Day.'

But ruining her *Christmas with this secret was clearly okay.* She caught Crispin studying them with a hint of trepidation.

'Right. I need my kitchen back.' Lowena clapped her hands. 'Anyone who isn't baking needs to find somewhere else to be.'

'I'll take Rhys to our room for a while. We have presents to wrap.' Samira wasted no time in whisking the protesting boy away from his father. That gave Ashley the chance to make a grab for him instead.

'It's unpacking time.'

'Lowena's scary,' he muttered under his breath as they collected his bags from the hall and headed upstairs. 'It baffles me how she and Nessa are so bloody different.'

'Ah, but you should've seen her the other night.' She giggled. 'She was as nervous as a cat on a hot tin roof when she went on a date.'

'A date?' Crispin raised an eyebrow. 'Who was brave enough to ask her out?'

'Don't be unkind.' Ashley jabbed him in the ribs. 'It was Terry Nancarrow, the craft gin distiller from Probus. Now I know why she was always hanging around his stall at the festival … looking for free samples.' Her suggestive wink made him chuckle. 'He seems a decent enough guy. Laid-back but not a doormat, if that makes sense.'

He followed her into the bedroom and set his backpack on the floor. They'd left the rest of his belongings in the storeroom.

'A bit like me then?'

'You?' Laid-back wasn't a description that sprang to mind when she thought about him. There was an intensity about everything he did; even when making love, his attention was totally focused. 'Hardly. You definitely aren't a doormat though, and I should know because I used to be one.'

'Used to be maybe, but not any longer. You're the strongest woman I know.' A shadow flitted over his smile. 'By the way, what was Samira on about when she collared you in the kitchen? It looked serious to me.'

She was glad they weren't face to face because then she wouldn't be able to lie. 'Oh, nothing much. She was asking if I thought Rhys was too young for the remote-control car her parents are getting him.'

'Oh right.' Crispin smirked back over his shoulder. 'Is this the bed you were boasting about?'

'I sure don't see any other.'

'Well, I think my unpacking can wait for a while. This can't.'

Ashley squealed when he scooped her up in his arms, stifled her shrieks with a lengthy kiss and deposited her on the bed.

'Nap time.'

'Uh, that implies sleep.'

'Yep.' His smouldering gaze dragged over her. 'After.'

Christmas clearly came early in Cornwall.

Chapter Twenty-Six

Crispin's skin numbed as he pressed his face against the window. The sight spread out in front of him was very different from the predicted Christmas Eve forecast. Overnight, a thick layer of snow had turned the front lawn into a white blanket, reminding him of childhood Christmases in Wales. Probably his memory tricked him but it seemed they were always snowy and perfect for sledding down the nearest hill on whatever they could find. Sheets of thick cardboard. Metal trays. Scraps of wood roughly nailed together. He and his friends would watch with envy as some of the richer boys zoomed past them on proper sleds.

'Oh wow. I didn't expect this.' Ashley wriggled in beside him. 'Y'all lied when you said you never got white Christmases.'

'It's rare. I was listening to the radio while you were still sleeping and heard on the news it's the first one in Cornwall since 2004. The temperature's been dropping all week, but they still didn't predict this. This will mess up a lot of people's Christmas plans.' A trickle of guilt slipped in because it'd just occurred to him that he'd escape making a fool of himself if tonight's show by the Wheal Boys was cancelled.

'Will the roads get cleared? We're useless in Tennessee. Anyone who moves down our way from up north laughs at us because the schools close at the first flake of snow and people swarm to the grocery stores as if they're preparing for Armageddon.'

'Sorry but it's bloody terrible here too from what I've heard people say. We haven't had any snow worth talking about since I've lived here. Most of the time though it apparently melts as fast as it arrived, but this looks ominous to me – we could be stuck.' Crispin nuzzled a kiss into her silky hair, which smelled wonderfully of ripe peaches. 'Wouldn't that be terrible?'

'Yeah, awful – but don't get too happy because I bet any minute now Lowena will be up here banging on the door. You'll be handed a shovel and told to clear the drive and I'll be roped in to cooking gallons of soup or whatever she reckons is essential.' Her smile softened. 'And you'll have to build a snowman for Rhys. That's compulsory.'

'Have I told you recently how much I love you?'

'You did mention somethin' on those lines last night when we were … you know?' A heated blush crept over her skin.

'I might need you to spell it out. My brain's on the slow side this morning.'

'Wicked man.'

'Are you awake?' Lowena shouted into them. 'Have you seen the weather?'

'Yeah, and we'll be down in a few minutes.'

'Good. We've got work to do.'

Crispin clutched her to his chest to stifle the giggles he felt bubbling inside her, but at the sound of Lowena's retreating footsteps he let go and they both burst out laughing.

'Are you still glad you moved in?'

'Absolutely.' He'd never taken this big a leap before with any woman, but it didn't feel in the least bit strange to see his sparse selection of clothes hanging next to hers in the wardrobe and their toothbrushes side by side in the bathroom across the hall.

'Me too.' She puffed an exaggerated sigh. 'We'd better get busy preparing for the apocalypse.'

Crispin reluctantly let her go, and for once she beat him getting dressed.

'I'm nabbing the bathroom first to wash my face then it's all yours. I'll see you downstairs.' Over by the door, she threw him an outrageous wink. 'Slowpoke.'

If they weren't in a hurry, he'd make Ashley pay him back for that in a fun way – but knowing he'd have the chance again tonight broadened his smile.

'So, what's the plan?' Ashley breezed into the kitchen and headed straight for the coffeepot. Lowena had finally conceded that she'd never convert her to the so-called delights of hot tea and made sure there was always hot coffee brewing by breakfast time. 'I'll miss you spoiling me this way.'

'You'll have to train Crispin.'

'He's not a pet monkey.'

'No, I'm more a cuddly teddy bear.' Two strong arms clamped around her waist. For a sturdy man, he was incredibly stealthy.

'You're goin' to give me a heart attack if you keep doing that.'

'Not part of the plan. I'd miss you too much.' Crispin reached for the frying pan. 'Bacon sandwiches sound good?'

It was typical of him to toss out a romantic remark then follow it with something down to earth and practical.

'Stupid question.'

Soon the kitchen filled with the best fragrance on earth.

'I'll walk out to the road and see how bad the snow looks.' Crispin polished off his breakfast standing up.

'I've spoken to the lady who took over the lunch club in the village and she's concerned about several of the members who live alone.' Lowena poured herself another cup of tea. 'I volunteered you and Ward to check on them because his truck will handle the dicey roads.'

'No problem.'

His swift agreement stopped Ashley from protesting that her friend should have checked with the men first before offering their services. To make up for her lack of graciousness, she offered to help make food for them to take. 'Soup maybe?' Out of the corner of her eye she caught Crispin's smirk.

'Perfect. When we've got it ready, Ward can drive up to collect Crispin and the food. It's lucky we bought all those thermos flasks for our houseguests' packed lunches. I've already taken bread rolls out of the freezer and mince pies.' Satisfaction oozed through her voice. 'All that extra baking we did is coming in handy.'

'Daddy, we have snow!' Rhys raced in, grinning from ear to ear.

Behind the little boy's shoulder, Ashley caught Samira's frown. No doubt it was on her mind that their plan to leave the day after tomorrow could be affected.

'I promised him we'd build a snowman.' Samira caressed her son's dark curls and smiled at Crispin. 'You could help.'

'I'd love to later, but I've got work to do first I'm afraid.'

She appreciated it when Lowena hurriedly explained the

situation so Samira wouldn't jump to the conclusion that Ashley was involved in stopping him.

'If I don't make it back from the North Pole soon, send out a search party.' He dragged on his coat and a woolly hat, and a blast of Arctic air chilled the room when he flung open the back door.

The kitchen immediately became a hive of activity – its usual status these days – leaving no time to dwell on what a strange Christmas Eve this was turning out to be.

'This is the last one.' Crispin jumped out of the truck and Ward passed over the thermos and bag of food. They'd delivered meals, shovelled paths and made sure everyone was safe and warm. 'Jigger Wallace, right?'

'Yeah. Nessa warned me the old guy is misery so don't expect a rapturous reception.'

'No worries.' Crispin trudged up to the old granite cottage but no one answered when he knocked. He walked around to bang on the back door with a similar lack of luck and a trickle of uneasiness crept through him. In the army he'd learned to pay attention to his instincts, so he hurried straight back to the truck. 'There's no sign of life. What do you reckon? Could he be with family or friends?'

'Shouldn't think so.'

'Reckon we should break in?' After a heartbeat's hesitation, Ward nodded. It was a relief when he discovered the door was unlocked so they wouldn't need to take any extreme measures. 'Jigger, we've brought some food from the lunch club. All right if we come in?' Silence. Inside the dark, narrow hall, he fumbled for the light switch then swore.

A bald, wizened man lay sprawled at the bottom of the stairs. Crispin crouched down and pressed a finger to the side of his neck then frowned over his shoulder at Ward. 'There's a pulse but it's weak. It'll take too long to get an ambulance in this weather. Stay with him while I track down Doc Thomas. Get a blanket to cover him up with but don't move him.' He registered Ward's faint smile. 'Sorry. Didn't mean to order you around.'

'Hey, you can take the guy out of the army but—'

'It's okay.' Crispin shrugged. 'I'll be as quick as I can.' He rushed as fast as he could along the street and dodged a group of kids enjoying a snowball fight. There was no sign of life in the surgery, but he rang the bell and a wave of relief washed over him when a youngish man with tousled blond hair opened the door. Crispin explained who he was and that they needed his help. 'Jigger Wallace had a fall.'

'I'll get my bag.'

The few minutes it took to walk back down the road together gave him time to fill the doctor in on the details as far as he knew them, and he was impressed by the man's friendly but no-nonsense attitude. Neither of them expected to step into the cottage and see the old man propped up with his back to the stairs.

'He came around shortly after you left and tried to get up but I ordered him to stay put.'

'Bleddy know it alls sticking yer noses in my business.' Jigger glowered at Ward.

'You should be thanking them for saving your life.' The doctor wagged his finger. 'You could've died and no one would've known.'

'Or cared.' Jigger threw another venomous look.

Crispin's sympathy was roused; he knew only too well what it was like to feel that way.

'They said you were out cold so you might have a concussion.' Dr Thomas sounded more sympathetic now.

'I were resting me eyes, that's all.'

'So, you let us worry while you took forty winks?' Crispin didn't believe that for one minute.

'Well, I might've been out a few seconds I 'spose.' That concession was hard won. 'I tripped over the damn cat and missed the last couple of steps.'

The doctor asked more questions and ran his hands over the old man. 'There's nothing broken so I think it's safe if we help him up. Let's take him in the kitchen where the light's better.' The full verdict didn't take long. 'You'll have some nasty bruises tomorrow but it's the possibility of a concussion I'm most concerned about. You can't stay here alone tonight. Is there anyone you can ask—'

'No.'

'It's not a problem, doc.' Ward intervened. 'He can stay with us at the farm. We've got a couple of spare bedrooms and my mother was a nurse so he'll be in good hands. If that's all right with you, Mr Wallace?'

'Don't suppose I've got a choice.' Jigger's grumbling had no heart to it.

'That's his way of thanking you.' The young doctor rolled his eyes.

'Do you want me to get your pyjamas and anything else you need?' Crispin took the man's grunt as agreement and headed upstairs.

Before long they'd loaded Jigger, his cat and a small overnight bag in the truck.

'Off we go to the Pear Tree Farm hotel.' Ward chuckled.

In the rear-view mirror, Crispin caught Jigger's faint smile.

Chapter Twenty-Seven

If she wasn't careful Crispin would catch her in the middle of her present wrapping ordeal. Ashley dragged out the shopping bags from the top shelf of the wardrobe and spread her purchases on the bed. This was the result of leaving things until the last minute. Distinctly unoriginal gifts.

Crispin recently admitted he needed to buy new clothes but hated shopping for them so she'd picked out several jumpers and shirts plus three smart pairs of trousers. She also raided the largest bookshop in Truro for a few titles he'd mentioned wanting to read and tracked down a new pair of his favourite brand of sturdy leather work boots. The only present she suspected would excite him had been delivered straight to Pear Tree Farm and was hidden in an outbuilding Ward had promised that no one ever used, ready to produce after lunch tomorrow.

She was no Kirstie Allsopp when it came to wrapping – the famous Brit was Lowena's creative guru – so the whole process didn't take long and she soon had the presents arranged under the tree. Voices drifted out from the kitchen and she found Lowena doling out cups of hot chocolate to the shivering snowman brigade. 'How did it go?' Ashley peered out of the window. 'Oh boy, that's the biggest one I've ever seen.' The towering figure stood in the middle of the lawn, proudly showing off its quirky combination of a ladies' straw summer hat complete with plastic daisies and a long red cape. Ashley's contribution was the Cornish tartan scarf knotted around its neck.

'Kit and Lucy were awesome.' Samira beamed at them. 'I'm not sure who enjoyed building it the most – them or Rhys.'

It was heart-warming to see the house coming to life this Christmas. Last year, she, Ward and Nessa sat around the farmhouse kitchen table and shared a small turkey breast, but tomorrow would be radically different. The dining room would strain joyfully at the seams, especially with an extra guest thanks to Crispin and Ward's rescue of old Mr Wallace. The original plan was to open their stockings here at Tregereth then take the rest of their presents down to Pear Tree Farm to delve into after lunch, but the unexpected snow had forced them to modify that. They'd open the majority of their gifts here and just carry one small present down to open along with everyone else.

'Are you and Crispin coming to the carol service?' Lowena handed her a steaming mug topped with a cloud of marshmallows.

'Will they still hold it?'

'Of course. It's Christmas Eve. You know it's going to be in the church hall? I can't remember if I told you the vicar was thrilled with the money they managed to raise at the festival. It's enough to start the church roof repairs in the New Year.'

'That's great. I'm glad we could help. And, yeah, we were planning to be at the service.'

'Afterwards we'll eat supper in the pub and—'

'Hear my daddy sing.' Rhys bounced up and down.

It hadn't been a surprise this morning when the Wheal Boys called to say they were marooned in Redruth and had to cancel their appearance at The Chough tonight. Crispin's relief had been replaced by stunned disbelief when her dear brother told Benjy Martin that the two of them would be happy to put on something instead so as not to disappoint people.

'I recommend hot baths all around then we'll find a Christmas film to watch.' Lowena's suggestion went down well and everyone finished their drinks before disappearing in a buzz of happy chatter. 'Crispin will be fine, you know? We'll all be there.'

That's the problem, she thought.

'Brooding doesn't do any good unless you're a chicken.' The witty declaration made her smile. 'Here you go.' Lowena shoved a peeler in her hand. 'I promised Nessa we'd prepare the veg for tomorrow's lunch. That means we need enough potatoes, carrots and sprouts for a dozen people.'

'Yes, ma'am.'

They worked away steadily until Lowena's mobile struck up the 'Joy to the World' ringtone she'd swapped to for the festive season.

'It's the vicar,' she mouthed. 'Yes, Peter what can I—' She went quiet. 'Oh dear, that's a shame – but there's no question of cancelling. We'll have to find a new venue, that's all. Give me five minutes and I'll ring you back.' Lowena ended the call. 'Well now there's a problem with the church hall roof of all things. One side has caved in under the weight of all the snow so we need somewhere else to hold the carol service.' A gleam lit up her bright blue eyes. 'I've got a brilliant idea and I'm sure Nessa won't mind. It's for the village.'

'Nessa?'

'Yes. We'll have it in her barn. What could be more perfect? It'll be exactly like the first Christmas.'

Ashley smiled through the ensuing phone call. She caught enough of Nessa's end of the conversation to pick up on her dismay before there was a thin attempt to come up with an alternative solution, but then her sister-in-law caved in. Like no one saw *that* coming.

'I'll ring the vicar to tell him then we'll all come down to help set up.' Lowena ended the call with a triumphant smile. 'Nessa thinks it's a super plan. I've told her to put Crispin and Ward to work straight away.'

'I'll go tell everyone what's happening.'

'Good girl.'

Ashley surprised Lowena with a hug. 'You are too. The best.'

The difference between Crispin's Christmas this year and last was huge. He'd spent the holidays on duty at the almost-deserted barracks in Plymouth, and apart from a quick phone call with Rhonda and a traditional turkey lunch, it could have been any day on the calendar. Tonight he looked forward to seeing his son's excitement when Rhys hung up his stocking, then sharing Ashley's bed again and tomorrow would also be awesome. He'd gained a new perspective on life these days making it possible to accept – at least most days – that everything he'd seen, done and endured in the army was merely one piece of the jigsaw puzzle of his life.

'I'll be off now.' He rinsed out his mug and left it on the dish rack to dry. 'See you at the carol service later.'

'Yeah, and thanks for helping get Jigger settled.' Ward rolled his eyes. 'The old guy's latched onto my dad and they're in the other room rehashing D-Day. Turns out they're both World War Two buffs.'

'Oh, I'm glad you haven't left yet.' Nessa hurried in and flicked anxious glances at them both. 'I've got new orders from Lowena. You're staying here.'

'But Ashley's expecting me back.' Crispin protested.

'Not now she isn't.'

A couple of minutes later he wasn't the only one bewildered.

'Seriously?' Ward stared at his wife in disbelief. 'You've agreed we'll turn the barn into an impromptu church in less than two hours?'

'Lowena was very … persuasive. What else could I do? Anyway, it's Christmas Eve and it's a village tradition so we can't—'

'Hey, it's okay sweetheart. I didn't mean to sound unwilling.' He raised an eyebrow at Crispin. 'We'll pull something together, won't we?'

'Yep. No problem.'

'Lowena and the others are heading this way soon to help out,' Nessa explained.

'Ask her to bring any spare Christmas lights she can find and get Kit to chop down a whole lot of holly branches.' Crispin clapped a hand on Ward's shoulder. 'Let's get on it.'

They grabbed their coats and headed to the barn.

'Any idea where to start?' Ward frowned at him.

'We need to get the festival stalls shifted outside and covered up to make more room. It's lucky we've got all those folding chairs.' He spotted the bales of straw left over from the Halloween maze. 'Those will be perfect for kids to sit on. There's nothing much we can do about it being cold in here, and even if we rounded up a ton of heaters most of the hot air would end up in the rafters. We'll put the word out for people to dress warmly.'

'We could move the Christmas tree in from the house to cheer things up a bit?'

'Not a bad idea.'

'Lowena's goin' to ask Jago if he can bring the animals for the live nativity scene here instead, although knowing her she won't give him much choice!' Ward chuckled. He pointed to the far corner of the barn. 'We could corral them there with some of the temporary fencing we used around the festival games.'

'That'll work. You start on that and I'll tackle the rest.'

'I've been sent to be another pair of hands.' Ward's father ambled in. 'Nessa's comin' too because Fiona's on Tristan duty.' He grinned. 'Real hardship.'

Half an hour later, everyone had arrived and it was all-hands-on-deck.

'How's it goin'?'

Crispin fought with his powers of self-restraint when Ashley appeared in front of him dressed from head to toe in red, smelling wonderful and looking extremely kissable. 'Where's Lowena?'

'Are you worried she'll try to take over?'

'No, because I have a cunning plan.'

'You've been watching too much *Blackadder*.'

He'd got her addicted to the old Rowan Atkinson comedy and now they routinely traded quotes. 'Watch this.' Crispin plastered on a smile and headed for Nessa's sister. 'Just the woman I was looking for. We're taking care of the grunt work, but could you be in charge of making it all look less bleak? The holly and the lights and whatever? Kit and Lucy can help.'

'Of course. Leave it to me.' She patted his arm and strode off.

'Genius.'

'Do I get a reward? A kiss maybe?'

'Later.' Her husky whisper about killed him. 'I'm going to help Ward carry the Christmas tree over. Keep your eye on the mission, soldier.'

'I'd say we've done a pretty awesome job.' Ashley linked arms with Crispin and her brother. Flanked by the rest of the contingent, everyone was taking a minute to admire the results of their hard work.

The barn's rough oak beams were draped with thick boughs of holly speckled with fat bunches of bright red berries and wrapped with strands of all the mis-matched fairy lights they'd been able to lay their hands on. They'd arranged the bales of hay so the children could see everything that was going on, and the farmhouse Christmas tree now took pride of place behind a portable electric keyboard organ belonging to Lucy, Kit's girlfriend.

Sudden baaing noises from the back of the barn made everyone laugh.

'Noel and Rudolph agree.' Jago laughed over at them. He'd brought newly born twin lambs with their mother, a disgruntled donkey and a baby calf.

'Oh my goodness, what wonderful people you are.' The vicar made his way down the makeshift aisle, and, from his stunned expression, was struggling to take it all in. 'Lowena, you've done an incredible job.'

'I haven't done much.' She pointed to Crispin and Ward. 'These two are the ones you've got to thank.'

'And I do. Very much. I've brought the service leaflets.' The vicar opened his backpack. 'People are starting to head this way from the village but I'm not sure how many will turn up. I warned them it'll be cold and some won't be able to get here anyway because the outlying areas are still pretty much cut off.' He waved at a grey-haired woman who'd just arrived and was taking off her coat. 'We can't do without our organist. I knew it would take more than a few inches of snow to put Miss Dowrick off.'

Ashley tugged on Crispin's hand. 'Let's find a seat. We've done our bit.'

The vicar took up his place at the front and welcomed everyone to their makeshift gathering before the first notes of 'Hark the Herald Angels Sing' rang out. Crispin's deep, rich voice. The pungent smell of the animals. Little children's excited chatter. The sparkling lights illuminating the barn and reminding her of the star-lit sky on that first Christmas. Everything combined to make Ashley's eyes sting with happy tears. The brief service flew by and Crispin draped his arm around her shoulders when they stood for the last carol, 'Silent Night'. A brief hush fell as the song ended then everyone started to talk again.

'Daddy, I want to pet the donkey.' Rhys tugged on his leg.

'Then let's do it.' He swept his son in his arms and Ashley experienced a brief flash of apprehension. The burden of knowing that Crispin's time with his son was dwindling away ate at her. What would happen if he couldn't forgive her deception?

'I've sent Kit and Lucy on to save us a couple of tables at the pub.' Lowena frowned at her. 'Are you all right?'

'Yeah. A bit tired, that's all.'

'If you say so.'

Ashley turned away as Crispin's arm snaked around her waist.

'We're ready. Jago's loading the animals up. Nessa says she'd giving the pub a miss to stay and put Tris to bed. She'll turn all the lights off in here when everyone's gone and lock up.'

'Let's go then.'

They linked hands and joined the rest of their cheerful group. The snow crunched under their feet, and all around the village Christmas lights glowed, competing with the stars piercing the clear, dark winter sky. Crispin stopped and drew her close for a kiss.

'I love you so much.' His thick, husky voice stirred her.

'And I love you too.' This was all she needed for Christmas.

Crispin was doing okay until he stepped inside the pub and spotted the wall-to-wall people crowded into the bar.

'You can do this,' Ashley whispered.

He managed to nod and raised a hand to Lowena who was waving at them across the packed room. They squeezed their way in through and sat next to Polly and Jack. He hadn't been sure if they'd feel up to coming tonight but was pleased to see them. Polly's freshly dyed bright green hair was a reassurance that she was feeling more like her old self again.

'What're you orderin'?'

Crispin waved away the menu Ashley was offering him. 'I'm not hungry. I'll get something later.' The fleeting longing for a whisky to settle his nerves ran through him when Ward was gathering up the drink orders.

'We'll both have soda and lime,' she answered for them before he could speak.

'You don't have—'

'It's what I want.' The fierce smile she flashed his way dared him to challenge her.

While everyone was busy eating, Crispin's stress level rose.

'Ready to go set up?' Ward caught his eye across the table.

'Yep.' His anxiety flattened out as if someone had clicked their fingers. It was always this way. When it was time for action, he had no problem focusing on that and nothing else. He noticed Ashley's surprise when he smiled and jumped up to join her brother. They still had a lot to learn about each other. Their relationship reminded him of being a child and going on old-fashioned mystery bus trips with his parents where the journey was as much a part of the experience as the final destination.

The hastily formed plan they'd made was to start with them singing a few old Cornish carols together before Ward performed a couple of Cornish mining songs alone. There was a powerful history behind the music his friend had chosen because much of it involved the "Cousin Jack" miners who left to find employment in mines all over the world, including one of Ward's ancestors. After that Crispin would take the lead on some Welsh carols. His friend had been fascinated to hear about the strong male voice choir tradition that originated with the coal miners, its harmonies and roots mirroring that of similar Cornish music coming from the region's own miners and fishermen.

When Ward reached the end of his part, Crispin launched into 'Cwm Rhondda' – the Welsh language version of 'Bread of Heaven'. Despite the fact it wasn't a Christmas song, he still got the noisiest audience participation of the evening. They wrapped up with one of Ward's discoveries – the old Newlyn carol titled 'The Carnal and the Crane'. Its haunting tune brought a hush to the crowded room before the applause started.

'Thanks for puttin' up with us, and Merry Christmas.' Ward raised his glass and everyone cheered.

A brief flutter of panic engulfed him when people swarmed around to congratulate them, but Ashley materialised by his side and inserted herself between him and the crowd. She understood that one reason he'd settled to working at Pear Tree Farm was the opportunity to spend most of his days outdoors. If mild claustrophobia was the worst lingering effect of his army days, Crispin could deal with that.

'There's some bloke outside looking for you.' Jago Teague tapped his shoulder.

'Does he have a name?'

'I asked but he wouldn't say. He's not local and looks a bit rough.' He shrugged. 'I tried to bring him in but he wouldn't come.'

'We'll go out.' Crispin grabbed her hand.

Their group had migrated towards the door and were debating who would ride in the truck with Ward who'd driven to transport their music gear.

A man emerged from the shadows and Crispin immediately recognised Chalky White's troubled features. The Royal Marine looked worse than he remembered. His straggly beard grazed his chest and his dark eyes were reduced to hollows. The soles were flapping on the poor guy's boots and he shivered through his thin nylon jacket.

'Sorry to bother you. I don't want to cause any trouble.' His voice was barely audible. 'I didn't know where else to go.' Chalky swayed on his feet, and Crispin and Ward managed to catch hold of him as he lurched forward.

'It's all right. We've got you. You're safe now.' There might not have been any room at the inn in the original nativity story, but things were different here.

'We'll take him to the farm,' Ward said. 'I reckon "Mr Blue Sky" needs a new occupant.'

Emotion tightened Crispin's throat. 'C'mon mate. Let's get you in the warm and find you a bite to eat.' Before he could apologise to Ashley for spoiling what remained of Christmas Eve, she wrapped her hands around his face and kissed him.

'I'll be waiting at home when you've settled your friend.'

They'd talked about Chalky often, and she knew his lingering sense of guilt over not being able to do more to help the troubled young man, but Christmas was a time for redemption.

Chapter Twenty-Eight

'Do you want to see what's in your stocking?' Ashley trailed a finger over Crispin's stubbly chin and smiled when he startled in his sleep. She should really leave him to rest; it'd been late when he finally got to bed – but if they didn't snatch a few moments alone now, Christmas Day would disappear in a puff of smoke.

'Yep, and hopefully the answer is you.' His muscular arms snaked around her, yanking her back against his warm, hair-roughened chest. 'Happy Christmas.'

'Someone sounds cheerful.'

'Why wouldn't I be? I've got a beautiful, naked woman in my bed, and she's just made me an amazing offer involving stockings.' He danced a hand along her thigh.

'Stocking. Singular. As in the Christmas variety.' She giggled and shifted away.

'Aren't we opening them downstairs together?'

'We could.'

'But?'

'You might not want your innocent son seeing some of the things Santa's sneaked into yours.' Ashley slipped out of bed to grab the two red velvet stockings laid on the floor. Yesterday she'd handed him the one with her name on and pretended to be asleep when he was furtively scrambling around filling it last night. 'Merry Christmas.' His face turned redder than the stocking as he pulled out a black lace bra and panties, black suspender belt and silk stockings. Underneath that were a few respectable gifts of chocolate and nuts, then she'd tucked a pair of black silk boxer shorts all the way down in the toe. 'Modelling time, I think.' She peeled off her pyjamas before wriggling into the almost-invisible panties. Teasing him was a piece of cake, and by the time she finished snapping the stockings in place his breathing had turned ragged. 'What about your shorts?'

'What about them? They'll be in the way. I'll let you enjoy them second time around.'

'Second?'

'Yep. In a nod to trans-Atlantic relations, I'm thinking we'll make love once for Father Christmas and then for Santa Claus.' Crispin's rumbling laughter filled the room. 'I assume you're in the festive mood this morning?' He hesitated. 'Oh, do you want to see what's in your stocking first? I'll warn you now, there's nothing as good as you've come up with.'

'It can wait.' She allowed her hand to trail downwards. 'I'm not waiting any longer for you.' Ashley opened her arms to him.

It almost unmanned Crispin when Rhys buried his small, warm body into his chest.

'They're 'xactly like yours, Daddy.' He took off striding around the room, showing everyone his new miniature-sized tan leather work boots. 'I can do jobs with you now.'

'You certainly can.' He refused to spoil Christmas moping over how quiet it'd be when the boy left. Ashley was settled on the floor by his feet resting her head against his legs, and he stroked her soft blonde hair while he gazed around and soaked up the day to add to the best of his memories.

Kit hauled out two boxes from under the tree and

pushed them towards Ashley. 'I reckon he's bought you a load of rocks.' They all knew it was making Lowena's day to have her son here and tomorrow he'd been persuaded to do Christmas all over again with his father.

Ashley studied the gift. 'Don't tell me present wrapping is another of your talents?'

'Definitely not. Thank the shop.'

She untied the wide blue ribbon and tore off the thick white paper. 'Oh.' Her hand flew to her mouth. 'You paid attention.'

'I try to.' A prickle of embarrassment crept up his neck when she lifted out a dinner plate and ran her fingers over the thick blue and white stripes. She delved into the other boxes, and by the time everything was spread around her on the carpet, there were tears glistening on her cheeks.

'You're a keeper.' Lowena beamed over at him. 'Now she won't complain when I take mine away. If we're all done, it's time we got ready to leave. Remember to wrap up warm.' The warning made everyone smile. 'Crispin and Kit – when you're ready, come to the kitchen and I'll have the food bags ready for you to carry.'

He almost saluted her.

The sun was peeking out as their gang set off down the snowy drive. According to the forecast, the temperature would start to warm up later in the day and he guessed the worst of the snow would've melted by morning. As Pear Tree Farm came into view, Crispin had the overwhelming sense of being a small part of the history of the old house and all of the Christmas celebrations it'd seen over the years.

'Happy Christmas.' Ward stood on the doorstep holding

Tristan in his arms with Nessa and his parents crowded around him.

'Oh my goodness, how adorable is our sweet boy!' Ashley pointed to the baby's green and red elf onesie.

'You've just beaten Polly and Jack. Here they are.'

His old friends arrived and a round of laughter ensued as they all admired the strand of miniature fairy lights wound around Polly's tower of bright green hair.

'Have you seen Chalky this morning?' Crispin asked. 'I don't like to think of him on his own, but I'm pretty sure we'd all be a bit much for him today.'

'He's all right. I checked.' Jack nodded. 'I told him we'd bring a plate of dinner up later.'

'Jigger is inside, hunched over the fire and moaning about his arthritis.' Ward chuckled. 'I don't think the old guy will want to go home again. He already reckons the sun shines out of my darling wife.'

Don't we all? thought Crispin with a smile.

They all piled into the house and Lowena clapped her hands to get everyone's attention. 'If you aren't helping with lunch, you need to stay out of the kitchen and the dining room.'

Crispin's stomach rumbled as the mouth-watering aroma of turkey roasting filled the hall. He didn't regret skipping breakfast though because Ashley's alternative offer had been head and shoulders above any bacon and eggs.

'There are some board games and puzzles in the living room and a few snacks to keep you going.'

When Lowena disappeared, Ashley pulled him to one side for a quick kiss. 'I'm on kitchen duty. Have fun.'

'Daddy, can you play with me?'

Crispin patted his son's dark curls. 'I sure can. Let's see what we can find.' Soon they were engrossed in a fierce game of Tiddlywinks, bringing back another childhood memory of playing with Rhonda when they were small. He'd never been one to make New Year's resolutions but silently promised to visit his sister soon and take Ashley and Rhys to meet her.

'Daddy, I don't want to play again. You be a horsey and I'll ride you.'

He slid down on all fours, playfully reared his head and snorted. 'Ride' em, cowboy!'

Ashley didn't need telling twice when Lowena insisted she'd done enough in the kitchen and followed Ward, who'd been dispatched to let everyone know they were ready to eat. Crispin was sprawled in a chair looking red in the face. 'What on earth have you been doing?'

'Rhys ran him ragged playing horse.' Samira held the tired little boy in her lap.

Perhaps she had done the right thing by agreeing to keep Samira's secret. He wouldn't be enjoying today so freely if he knew they were leaving tomorrow.

'Sounds like fun. Come on. Let's go stake a spot.'

They managed to sit together along one side of the long mahogany table that was covered from end to end with steaming platters of food.

Ward stood and tapped his spoon on a glass. 'Before we eat, I'm gonna tell a quick story. The first time I ate in this room was with Nessa and my folks, I pictured a Christmas tree standing in the corner by the window and all of our families gathered around. I even conjured up a baby in Nessa's arms with her dark hair and my grey eyes.'

Hearing her brother's thickening voice made Ashley's throat tighten with emotion.

'Today that dream has come true. I don't have the faintest idea why I've been blessed this way but I'm damned grateful.' He lifted his glass. 'Whether you're family, old friends or new ones, I hope y'all know how loved and welcome you are today. Now dig in and eat but make sure to save space for pudding.' He cracked a grin. 'I'm gettin' the hang of the British lingo, although I'm assured that today we actually do have a real pudding.'

Plates were passed around and loaded up, and the noise level came and went in waves as people talked and ate.

'I reckon we've done all the damage we can here.' Ward stood again. 'I've been told we're delaying the famous pudding because some people can't wait to open their presents.' He pointed a finger at Nessa. 'No names needed.'

They crowded into the living room and Crispin made a beeline for his same chair then swept Ashley onto his lap. Presents were ripped open and examined and the loudest laughs came when her parents received matching T-shirts from Nessa proclaiming them "Cornish by marriage".

Ashley beckoned Rhys over and whispered in his ear, telling him what to say. 'Daddy, you have to come outside for one of your presents.'

'Y'all can come and see too,' she told everyone and took the little boy's hand. 'Rhys is comin' with me to fetch it.' They hurriedly picked their way through the snow across to the outbuilding where she'd stored Crispin's present.

The little boy gawked at the gleaming red bicycle with a big red bow tied around the handlebars.

'Oh wow, is that for my daddy?'

'Yeah, and when you're bigger I'll get you one too.'

'Really?'

'Yep.'

They wheeled it over to the house and Crispin's eyes widened in disbelief as he stepped forward and ran his fingers over the frame.

'Ride it, Daddy,' Rhys begged.

'I'll have a go, but I can't go too far in the snow or I might wreck it.' He hopped on and made a cautious couple laps of the yard to everyone's cheers then slid off and came over to hug her. Crispin dragged a kiss over her mouth and lowered his voice to a whisper. 'I'm not the only one who pays attention when it comes to gift giving, am I? I'll thank you properly later.'

'I'll look forward to it.'

'Daddy, I don't like Christmas pudding but Nessa has chocolate ice cream with chocolate sauce 'specially for me. I'll share it with you.' Rhys tugged on his hand.

'That sounds awesome. We'll go in a minute.'

'We sure will miss this dear little boy and our sweet baby.' Fiona stroked Tristan's cheek, cuddling him closer. 'I suppose they'll be leaving soon? You sure will miss them.'

'I'm not sure when exactly they're going. We haven't talked about it.'

'We're going tomorrow, Mrs Spencer,' Samira said casually and Ashley's heart sunk. 'I've got lesson plans to work on before classes start next week.'

'Tomorrow?' Crispin's smile disappeared in a flash. 'Why didn't you tell me?'

'I wanted you to enjoy your first Christmas with Rhys. I honestly thought you knew by now anyway but had decided not to spoil things by talking about it yet.'

'Why on earth would you think I knew?'

Ashley tried to sneak a glare at Samira but he swung around and caught her out.

'Oh like that, is it? I'm too fragile for the truth so you ganged up behind my back?'

'No! That's so not true.'

'Really? That's what it looks like from where I'm standing. I'm going to see Chalky.' He stomped off.

'Oh Lord, I sure am sorry. I never meant to put my foot in it.' Fiona slapped a hand over her mouth. 'I've ruined everything.'

'No, Mom, you haven't.' Ashley hugged her mother. 'He'll be all right. I'll talk to him later.' She wasn't convinced but refused to make her mother feel any worse. 'Is it pudding time now?' She ruffled Rhys's hair. 'And I think someone wants ice cream. Come on. I'll race you inside.'

Happy Christmas to me, she thought.

Chapter Twenty-Nine

Stepping back into the familiar caravan reminded him of visiting his childhood school as a grown up when the building seemed half the size and he felt like a giant.

'Tea?' Chalky held up the kettle and inched out a smile. 'I'd offer you something stronger as it's Christmas but I don't touch the stuff any longer. Can't.'

'Me neither so don't worry. Tea's fine. You settling in okay?' There was a flash of pain in the marine's pale blue eyes before he turned away to make their tea. 'Daft question. I only stopped by to see if there was anything you needed.' That wasn't entirely true because he'd come as much for his own sake, leaving before he could say something else he'd regret. Of course now he saw he'd been a flat-out dick and would have to grovel big-time later. Samira had tried to make up for the Christmases he and Rhys had missed out on and all Ashley did was help. Fiona's stricken expression wouldn't leave him alone either. The poor woman hadn't expected her innocent remark to cause an uproar.

'Nah, I'm good.' Chalky gestured to a clean dinner plate on the counter. 'Nessa made sure I didn't go hungry and I had a warm bed to sleep in last night. It's more than a lot have.'

Crispin nodded. 'You've got great people around you here and they won't let you go under. I'm just up the road too. In a couple of days, we'll be back to normal routine then I'll show you around both places if you like. We can talk about what you can do to help out. That's how I tried to repay some of their hospitality and acceptance.'

'Works for me.' A long searching look came his way. 'I thought you'd be laying a lot of crap on me about going back to the Marines and setting the record straight.'

It wasn't crap, but he realised the young man's head wasn't in the right place to see it yet.

'You want milk and sugar in your tea?'

'Milk. No sugar.' He peered out of the window. 'Sun's out and the snow's starting to melt. Should be gone overnight.' Crispin kept his voice steady. 'That's good because my ex and our little boy are getting the train back to Shrivenham near Oxford in the morning.'

'You're lucky to have them.'

'Do your family know where you are?'

'Family? Don't have any. It's why I joined up in the first place. It was that or another fucking foster home.' Chalky shook his head. 'Bloody idiot I was. What made you join up?'

'There wasn't much in the way of jobs in Cardiff for sixteen-year-olds with no qualifications.' Crispin shrugged. 'I was shit in school but good with my hands and athletic. The army seemed a good fit.' He tried to be fair. 'I got a lot out of it before it ground me down.'

'You're in a good place now? In your head, I mean.'

'Yep. Took time though. Didn't happen overnight.' Making it sound easy wouldn't help. Crispin drained his tea. 'I ought to get a move on. Take care of yourself all right?'

'You too and thanks again.'

He headed out, leaving "Mr Blue Sky" to someone else in need of its special magic and set off to mend some bridges.

Outside the farmhouse he sucked in a few deep breaths and pushed open the door.

The following morning the snow was reduced to piles of grey slush, suiting the general mood of the day. Ashley's heart lodged in her throat as Crispin wrapped Rhys in one last tight hug.

'Remember I'll come to see you really soon.' He cradled his son's face in his broad hands. 'Anytime you want to talk to me, just tell your mummy and we'll chat. Okay?' The boy's sad nod tore at her. Crispin straightened as a car crunched over the gravel. He'd offered to drive them to the train station, but by mutual decision they decided it was easier on everyone to say their goodbyes here.

'Thanks for everything.' Samira gave her a weak smile. 'This hasn't been easy on any of us but you've been incredible. I'm not sure I'd have been so accepting.'

'I love Crispin and you're his family. It's a no-brainer.' That was the truth despite the fact it simplified a complicated situation.

Before they knew it the bags were loaded in the taxi and Crispin stepped away, linking arms with her while Samira and Rhys clambered in. As they drove away, the only sound came from a raucous seagull swooping overhead which set off the noisy crows in the nearby trees.

'You okay?' She had no idea why she'd asked such a dumb question. 'Sorry.'

'Don't be. There's no road map for how to act in these situations. We're all doing our best.' Crispin stroked a kiss on her mouth. 'Let's go inside. We're having supper with your parents, right?'

'Yeah, but we've got the day to ourselves before that because Kit's with his dad and Lowena's on another date with her gin man.'

'How's that romance going?'

'Good but slow. She's not rushing into anything.'

'Wise. Trust is a fragile thing but the strongest too if that makes sense?' His face fell. 'Sorry. I'm not trying to rehash the whole secret leaving thing with Samira. Honestly.'

'I know.' For a few stupid moments yesterday when Crispin had stormed off, she'd gone into a panic and allowed herself to forget it was him she was dealing with and not her jerk of an ex-husband. But he apologised to her in front of everybody for flying off the handle and assured her she had nothing to be sorry for. Then he did the same with Samira and made his peace with Fiona. That was the mark of a genuine, loving man. 'Do you think you should check on Chalky?'

'Yeah, but if we go down to the farm early tonight I'll slip up to see him while you enjoy some extra time with your parents.'

'And what're we goin' to do until then?' Ashley snaked her arms around his waist.

'You got something in mind?'

'Might do. Want to find out?' His eyes smouldered. This man was quick to catch on.

Ashley bit her lip to keep from crying. In the twinkling light of the Christmas tree her mother was curled up in Nessa's favourite dark red wingback chair cradling her sleeping grandson. 'You'll come back again soon.'

'Not soon enough.'

Out of nowhere she received a full-blown Mom stare. The kind that'd kept her and Ward in line growing up.

'Ashley Louise, don't you even think about it.'

'What?'

'Running back to Tennessee because you think your daddy and I can't cope without you and your brother. Ward's got his lovely family and you've met someone good enough to deserve you. You're not throwing it away to babysit us.'

'I promise I won't. I can't.' Her mother wouldn't expect her to apologise for telling the truth.

Her father poked his head in around the door. 'Am I interrupting one of those woman talks?'

Ashley laughed. 'No Daddy, you're safe.'

With that Crispin and Ward materialised behind him and all three men trooped in.

'Someone needs to go to bed, I'm afraid.' Ward headed towards his son. 'Nessa's got supper ready in the kitchen.' Their mother sighed, kissed the baby's head and passed him over.

'Were your ears burning?' She grinned at Crispin.

'Should they have been?'

'Only in a good way. I'll give you the details later.' She steered him from the room. 'Let's eat. Mom and Dad wanted pasties one more time. How was Chalky?'

'Not bad. Tomorrow I'll show him around and find him some work to do. Being idle won't help.'

'Is that the Crispin Davies counselling method?'

'He made a similar crack.' The good humour seeped from his face. 'Am I interfering where I shouldn't?'

'No.' Ashley shook her head. 'You're a kind-hearted man who's trying to help. One day he'll appreciate it.'

They followed the fragrant scent to the warm kitchen and squeezed into the two vacant chairs. That was the signal for everyone to start on their pasties and conversation was sparse until they all had clean plates

'That was good eatin'.' Her father patted his stomach and pushed his chair away from the table. 'We'll have to come back real soon for more of those.'

'You sure will, Dad.' Ward winked. 'Of course, we all know that's the only reason you'd want to bother. A certain baby's got nothin' to do with it.'

'Quite right.'

Her mother poked him in the ribs sharp enough to make her husband yelp.

'Y'all know he's lying. Neither of us is lookin' forward to leaving.' Fiona looked misty-eyed for a second. 'We'll miss you two as well.' She switched her attention over to her and Crispin. 'But now you've got each other, I'm easier in my mind.'

'Uh, Mrs Spencer.' Crispin looked flustered. 'I haven't mentioned it to Ashley yet but—'

'For a start, how many times have I told you to call me Fiona? And my girl won't appreciate it if you spill the beans about something personal.'

'It's not … I didn't mean … not now at least … I was thinking we might come and see you in Tennessee if we can get away for a fortnight or so?' When he turned to her, she noticed the tips of his ears were bright pink. 'You keep saying it's pretty in the spring. What do you think?'

She flung her arms around his neck and kissed him hard on the mouth.

'You like the idea?'

'No, this is me being cross and miserable. But what about work?'

'It's not a problem.' Ward grinned at them and Lowena swiftly rushed to agree. 'We can manage just fine. It'll help keep our new recruit busy too, if he doesn't do a disappearing act.'

'I hope he doesn't.' Crispin sounded serious.

'I'd love nothing better than taking you to Tennessee. It'll give me a chance to prove we've some springtime beauty to rival Cornwall.'

'Well, we'd love to see you both anytime you can make it across the pond.' Her mother's smile returned. 'Now, why don't we make coffee and take it in the other room to enjoy the Christmas decorations while we still can?'

And each other's company. That part didn't have to be spelled out.

Chapter Thirty

Four months later – April

'*Two* of Jack's cremated sausages? You're a martyr, Crispin Davies.'

'Must be to live with you.' He munched on the charcoal crusted meat. 'We're lucky with the weather.'

It'd been Nessa's idea to round up the Pear Tree Farm "family" to meet Polly and Jack's relatives who were visiting from Birmingham for the weekend. Their group included Jigger Wallace, who'd become one of them since his enforced stay over Christmas. The old man was the only one who relished Jack's cooking. *Go figure*, she thought. Ashley took a guess that having a meal put in front of him and not eating alone mattered far more than the actual food involved.

'Not that it would've been a problem because we could've re-enacted Christmas and set up in the barn.' A thoughtful look crept over his face. 'That could be another money-spinner, you know?'

'What could? Running carol services?'

Crispin rolled his eyes. 'No, but if we smartened up the barn we could hire it out for events. Weddings and stuff.'

Ashley couldn't help laughing. 'You're gettin' as bad as Lowena.' Becoming a partner in the business had given him so much more than simply a larger pay cheque at the end of the month. Self-respect had no price. 'I think it's genius though.'

'Hey mate, can I have a quick word?' Chalky hovered behind them. 'Somewhere quieter maybe?'

'Oh yeah, course you can.' He sprang up and steered the younger man away from the crowd.

She lazed back and watched little Tristan. Seven months old now and on the verge of crawling, he was sitting on a colourful blanket spread out on the grass surrounded by admirers.

'You lookin' forward to goin' home, Ash?' Ward handed her an open bottle of Rattler cider – a local brew that had become her favourite. 'I bet our folks are countin' the days.'

'I am too.'

'It was one of your better ideas to suggest bringing them back here with you afterwards.' He glanced towards his son. 'Tris is growin' so fast.'

'I hear it's what happens when you feed and water them.' Ashley sensed her brother's scrutiny. 'What?'

'Tell me to butt out of your business, but have you and Crispin talked about—'

'Are you and Nessa goin' to give Tris a little brother or sister soon?' she interrupted. His face set in a glare. 'Don't like the boot on the other foot, do you?'

Ward threw up his hands. 'Mouth zipped.'

'Keep it that way.'

Crispin dropped back down in the chair next to her and she noticed the tight set of his mouth.

'Is Chalky okay?'

'He will be.'

'Are you gonna explain or sit there bein' all enigmatic?'

'You make me sound like some old-time Hollywood film star.' His brief smile faded. 'Chalky's made up his mind to turn himself back in to the Royal Marines and take what's coming.'

'That's good right?' Ashley wasn't sure why he looked so down.

'Yes. I just know the tough road he's got ahead of him.'

She squeezed his hand. 'But right now he's always watching over his shoulder like you were.' His weary nod said it all. 'You've done your best. This part he's got to do on his own.'

'He's a hard worker and Ward and Nessa will miss him. It's lucky they've got Kit onboard for a few weeks on his spring holidays from college. He'll fill in the gap and I'll look at helping to find a permanent replacement when we get back from Tennessee.'

Ashley rested her head against his shoulder. 'I've got a feeling Chalky will be back. He's like us and carved himself a place and a home here.'

'Why're you so damn smart?'

'Smart? If I'm so smart, why do I love *you*?' He returned her brilliant smile. 'How about we escape and take a walk in the walled garden?' Ashley stood up and smoothed down her dress – a new lime and white linen shift she'd bought for their upcoming travels but impulsively decided to wear today.

'We can if you want.'

'Don't be grumpy or you'll turn into a younger version of Jigger.'

Crispin tilted her a sly smile. 'Hey, even he's mellowed so there's still hope for me.'

'Maybe.' She linked her arm through his. 'Let's find out.'

*

A pale gold light bathed the garden as the day faded towards dusk, and the drift of Ashley's perfume reminded him of ripe fruit as her warm body pressed against his. As they walked arm in arm, he pointed out the extra rows of vegetable seedlings Chalky had planted under Nessa's supervision that were more fodder for her garden-to-table plans.

'She's thinking of turning another section of the top field over too. It's not as sheltered, but that won't be a problem for the hardier plants. I've made a start on a vegetable plot at our place but I've got more plans for it.'

'I'm sure you do.' She reached up and kissed him, drawing her hands down his back. 'And I'd honestly love to hear all about them another time, but not right now.'

'You brought up the subject.'

'Oh Crispin, have the last few months taught you nothing?' Her lilting laugh sent tingles shooting straight to his core. 'I lured you here under false pretences.'

'Don't get me wrong. I'd enjoy nothing better than making love to you right now but—'

'That's not what I meant.' A wicked shine lit up her eyes. 'Although now you've lodged the idea in my brain, I can clearly see us bailing out of here early.'

'A private party for two works for me.'

'There's somethin' I want to ask you first though.' Her face resembled an inferno.

'Anything. You know that by now.'

'Let's sit down.'

They settled on the old wood bench Nessa's father had carved for her mother, situated in the perfect spot to survey the whole garden. The side of him that'd become a passionate gardener couldn't help noticing new growth on the famous pear trees and Chalky's freshly dug earth ready for the spring planting to start.

'Do you remember what you said to me once?'

'I've said a lot of stuff. Remind me.' Before she could reply a bolt of awareness struck and Crispin felt himself turn as white as his T-shirt. Ward and Nessa often bragged about the spot where he'd asked her to marry him, saying they should erect a plaque renaming it "The Proposal Bench".

'Oh God. I'm about to make a fool of myself, aren't I?' The wobble in Ashley's voice kicked his brief flicker of panic out the door.

'No!' Crispin seized her hands. 'I'm just bowled over that you want to ...' Was he making a fool of *him*self? 'I hope I don't have the wrong end of the stick?'

'What a pair we are.' Now her eyes positively danced. 'So much for us being honest and straightforward. Yes, I am tryin' to ask you to marry me. We agreed I would if I felt the time was right and, well, it's right where I'm concerned. So how about you?'

'He swept his gaze over her. 'You've forgotten something.'

'What?'

'You're supposed to get down on one knee and have a ring all ready.' Crispin worked on looking thoughtful. 'I suppose I could give you a pass on the ring part because I'm not much into jewellery, but I promise I'll buy you one before we go see your parents.'

'Fine.' Ashley huffed. 'Now I don't want to hear any more complaints.' She lifted her dress out of the way but he shot out a hand to stop her.

'Don't be daft, you'll ruin that pretty dress – and your knees! I'm joking. If you tell me how much you love me

208

and that you want to spend the rest of our lives together, that'll do.'

'Oh, will it! Aren't you the noble one?'

By now they were both laughing so hard they could barely breathe let alone speak. Crispin recovered first. 'Marry me,' he whispered.

'I asked first.'

'I'm happy to accept your offer if you'll do the same and accept mine in return.' He turned serious. 'A good marriage is fifty-fifty. Right down the line. That's what I want.'

'Me too.' Ashley's soft hair brushed his cheek. 'There's a ready-made party out there, so what do you say we join them and share the news?'

'Let's phone your mum and dad first.'

'And Rhonda.'

He nodded. 'She'll love you.' Crispin gave a wry smile. 'Of course she's bound to question how sensible you are for wanting to take me on.'

'That works both ways. Fifty-fifty, remember?'

'I won't ever forget.' The solemn promise made her eyes glaze over with unshed tears. 'All I hoped for when I first came to Pear Tree Farm was a sliver of peace, a breathing space, but I found so much more and you ... I could never have imagined or dreamed of you.'

'It's the same for me, and if ever anyone says we've nothing in common we'll know they don't have a clue what they're talkin' about.'

He held her close to savour the moment and her heartbeat fluttered against his own. Everything else could wait. They'd worked out what truly mattered and it was right here.

Thank You

I'm supremely thankful to the amazing Tasting Panel members who were happy to return to Pear Tree Farm for the festive season along with all of my lovely, loyal readers and give Ashley and Crispin their well-deserved chance at happiness. If you would like to help spread the word about *A Cornish Christmas at Pear Tree Farm* and have a minute to leave a review where you bought the book that would be amazing.

Angela

x

About the Author

Angela was born in St. Stephen, Cornwall, England.
After completing her A-Levels she worked as a Naval
Secretary. She met her husband, a US Naval Flight Officer
while being based at a small NATO Headquarters on
the Jutland Peninsula in Denmark. They lived together
in Denmark, Sicily, California, southern Maryland
and London before settling in Franklin, Tennessee.

Angela took a creative writing course in 2000 and
loved it so much that she has barely put her pen down
since. She has had short stories and novels published
in the US. Her debut novel, *Sugar & Spice*, won
Choc Lit's Search for an American Star competition.

Follow Angela:
Twitter: www.twitter.com/AngelaBritnell
Facebook: www.facebook.com/angelabritnell

More Choc Lit

From Angela Britnell

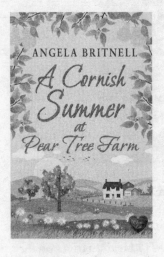

A Cornish Summer at Pear Tree Farm

Book 1 in the Pear Tree Farm series

Cornish charm and a Tennessee twist – the perfect pair?

Nessa Vivian is determined to keep her parents' business afloat, but Pear Tree Farm near the backwater Cornish village of Polgarth didn't do well as a farm, and it's not faring much better as a camp site. Maybe it's due to Nessa's habit of taking in troubled runaways, like ex-soldier Crispin, for next to nothing. Or perhaps her highly-strung sister Lowena is right – caravans named after Beatles' songs and homegrown pears are not enough to turn the farm into a tourist haven.

Then another troubled runaway turns up, posing the greatest threat yet. Ex-musician Ward Spencer from Tennessee is certainly intriguing, but could his plans to put nearby Tregereth House on the map mean Pear Tree Farm is finished – or does his arrival signal a second lease of life, and not just for Nessa's business?

Visit www.choc-lit.com for details.

Sugar and Spice

The Way to a Hero's Heart ...
Fiery, workaholic Lily Redman wants more
than anything to make a success of her new
American TV show, Celebrity Chef Swap –
without the help of her cheating ex-fiancé and
producer, Patrick O'Brien. So when she arrives
in Cornwall, she's determined to do just that.

What Happens in Nashville

'What happens in Nashville, stays in Nashville!'
Claire Buchan is hardly over the moon about
the prospect of her sister's hen party; travelling
from the UK to Nashville, Tennessee, for a
week of honky-tonks, karaoke and cowboys.
Certainly not Claire's idea of a good time, what
with her lawyer job and sensible boyfriend,
Philip.

But then she doesn't bank on meeting Rafe
Castello. As he and Claire get to know each
other, she realises there is far more to him than
meets the eye.

Celtic Love Knot

Can two tangled lives make a love knot?
Lanyon Tremayne is the outcast of his small
Cornish village of St. Agnes. Nobody knows the
painful secret he hides.

But when Olivia meets the ruggedly
handsome Lanyon, her trip to Cornwall looks
set to become even more interesting.

Visit www.choc-lit.com for details.

The Wedding Reject Table

Once on the reject table, always on the reject table?

When Maggie Taylor, a cake decorator, and Chad Robertson, a lawyer from Nashville Tennessee, meet at a wedding in Cornwall it's not under the best circumstances.

They have both been assigned to 'the reject table', alongside a toxic collection of grumpy great aunts, bitter divorcees and stuffy organists.

Here Comes the Best Man

Being the best man is a lot to live up to …

When troubled army veteran and musician Josh Robertson returns home to Nashville to be the best man at his younger brother Chad's wedding he's just sure that he's going to mess it all up somehow.

But when it becomes clear that the wedding might not be going to plan, it's up to Josh and fellow guest Louise Giles to make sure that Chad and his wife-to-be Maggie get their perfect day.

Love Me for a Reason

Love doesn't always have to make sense …

When Daisy Penvean meets Nathaniel Dalton whilst visiting a friend in Nashville, it seems there are a million and one reasons for them not to be together. Nathaniel's job as a mergers and acquisitions manager means sharp suits and immaculate hair, whereas Daisy's work as a children's book illustrator lends itself to a more carefree, laid-back style. And, as Daisy lives in England, there's also the small matter of the Atlantic Ocean between them.

Visit www.choc-lit.com for details.

You're The One That I Want

What if you didn't want to fake it any more?
When Sarah, a teacher from Cornwall, and Matt, a businessman from Nashville, meet on a European coach tour, they soon find themselves in a relationship …

Except it's a fake relationship. Because Matt is too busy for romance, and Sarah is only trying to make her cheating ex-husband jealous … isn't she?

Christmas at Black Cherry Retreat

What if you had nowhere to call home for Christmas?
When Fee Winter books a winter break at the remote Black Cherry Retreat in the small town of Pine Ridge, Tennessee, it's with the idea that the peace and quiet will help her recuperate from her hectic life as a photographer.

But what she didn't bank on was meeting Tom Chambers and his huge, interfering yet lovable family. With them, could Fee finally experience the warmth and support that's been missing from her own life?

One Summer in Little Penhaven

Could one summer change your life?
When high-flying American lawyer Samantha Muir finds out she's lost her partnership whilst on an assignment in London, she has a dramatic reaction.

Rather than returning home, she resigns, leaves her business suits behind and jumps on the first train to Cornwall at the encouragement of a friendly stranger.

Could the Cornish village and Cadan play a part in Samantha's summer of self-discovery?

Visit www.choc-lit.com for details.

Christmas in Little Penhaven

Have yourself a little Cornish Christmas ...
Wannabe author Jane Solomon is expecting an uneventful Christmas in her Cornish village of Little Penhaven.

But then super fit American gym owner Hal Muir comes to town, and suddenly the holiday season looks set to be far more interesting. Hal is keen on embracing every British tradition on offer, from mince pies to Christmas pub quizzes – and perhaps some festive romance too ...

New Year, New Guy

Out with the old life, in with the new ...
When Laura's bride-to-be sister, Polly, organises a surprise reunion for her fiancé and his long lost American friend, Laura grudgingly agrees to help keep the secret. And when the plain-spoken, larger-than-life Hunter McQueen steps off the bus in her rainy Devon town and only just squeezes into her tiny car, it confirms that Laura has made a big mistake in going along with her sister's crazy plan.

A Summer to Remember in Herring Bay

Essy Havers is good at finding things. But now Essy has something more important to find: herself
Essy has always been curious about her mother's secret past and her Cornish roots. So, when the opportunity arises, she hops on a plane in Tennessee and ends up in Herring Bay in Cornwall; the village where her mother grew up.

But once there, she's mystified by the reactions of the villagers when they realise who she is. Was Essy's decision to visit Cornwall a mistake, or will it lead to a summer she'll never forget?

Visit www.choc-lit.com for details.

Christmas at Moonshine Hollow

Mistletoe and moonshine: a Christmas match made in heaven?

Moonshine Hollow's famous 'Lightning Flash' might be an acquired taste, although the same could be said for moonshine distillery owner Cole Landon, what with his workaholic habits and 'Scrooge' tendencies when it comes to all things Christmassy.

But when Jenna Pendean from Cornwall pays a visit to Cole's family-run distillery in Tennessee during the holiday season, will Cole's cynicism about the existence of Christmas miracles be put to the test?

Spring on Rendezvous Lane

Can even the most seasoned traveller find a home on Rendezvous Lane?

'Community spirit' is not a phrase in travel junkie Taran Rossi's vocabulary. But a springtime stint house sitting for his grandmother on Rendezvous Lane in East Nashville could lead to a long overdue wake-up call. With the help of single mum Sandy Warner and her young son Chip, can Taran come to understand that sometimes it's not about the place – it's about the people?

Summer at Seaspray Cottage

What would you do if you inherited a Cornish cottage by the sea?

If you're Thea Armitage, sell it as soon as possible. Local bad boy Harry Venton played no small part in Thea's decision never to return to Cornwall twenty years before – and now he's her neighbour! Could things get any worse?

Except Harry isn't the boy he was, and as Thea comes to realise that her opinion of him was built on lies and misunderstandings, perhaps things will start looking up for her summer at Seaspray Cottage …

Visit www.choc-lit.com for details.

Introducing Choc Lit

We're an independent publisher creating
a delicious selection of fiction.
Where heroes are like chocolate – irresistible!
Quality stories with a romance at the heart.

See our selection here:
www.choc-lit.com

We'd love to hear how you enjoyed *A Cornish Christmas at Pear Tree Farm*. Please visit **www.choc-lit.com** and give your feedback or leave a review where you purchased this novel.

Choc Lit novels are selected by genuine readers like yourself. We only publish stories our Choc Lit Tasting Panel want to see in print. Our reviews and awards speak for themselves.

Could you be a Star Selector and join our Tasting Panel?
Would you like to play a role in choosing which novels
we decide to publish? Do you enjoy reading women's
fiction? Then you could be perfect for our Tasting Panel.

Visit here for more details…
www.choc-lit.com/join-the-choc-lit-tasting-panel

Keep in touch:
Sign up for our monthly newsletter Spread for all the latest
news and offers: www.spread.choc-lit.com.
Follow us on Twitter: @ChocLituk,
Facebook: Choc Lit and Instagram: @ChocLituk.

Where heroes are like chocolate – irresistible!